TINKI

Other Series by H.P. Mallory

Paranormal Women's Fiction Series:
Haven Hollow
Midlife Spirits
Midlife Mermaid

Paranormal Shifter Series:
Arctic Wolves

Paranormal Romance Series:
Underworld
Lily Harper
Dulcie O'Neil
Lucy Westenra

Paranormal Adventure Series:
Dungeon Raider
Chasing Demons

Detective SciFi Romance Series:
The Alaskan Detective

Academy Romance Series:
Ever Dark Academy

Reverse Harem Series:
Happily Never After
My Five Kings

TINKER

Book 6
The Happily Never After Series

By

HP Mallory

10 Chosen Ones:
When a pall is cast upon the land,
Despair not, mortals,
For come forth heroes ten.
One in oceans deep,
One the flame shall keep,
One a fae,
One a cheat,
One shall poison grow,
One for death,
One for chaos,
One for control,
One shall pay a magic toll.

Tinker:
Seelie extinguished,
scales unbalanced,
a lone light to guide the way.
She will depose the venal king and
reforge the future of the fae.

ONE
TINKER

I run my fingers along the curved pine wood of the *Little White Bird.* The wood stain is setting in nicely so the vessel has more dignity now than it did in the last few years. There's something sad, I believe, about naked wood on a sailing vessel.

Not that I think the *Little White Bird* will be doing any sailing in the near future, but a pixie can still dream. And I do—and have been my entire life.

The ship is easily three times my height and difficult to scale if I want to make it onto the deck without flying. Zegar likes to keep me flat-footed and traveling like a mortal. I suppose it makes sense, as I trail pixie dust when I fly and what could be more obvious than that? Still, it's chaffing to move like this, and it's slow, even after all these years. *Ten* at last count. Or is it eleven now? I'll have to check the tally marks on the mast.

Digging my fingers into the seams between the wood, I work my way up the keel until I can reach the edge of a gun port. Once I find purchase, it's a simple thing to swing myself up and over. I may flutter my wings, just once, letting a cascade of fine golden-green dust tinkle to the deck below. Zegar will spawn a

1

generation of hatchlings if he finds out what I'm up to. But, I just can't help it. I only have a few joys in this miserable place and I won't let Zegar steal another of them. Yes, he can be quite… boring.

The deck creaks lightly beneath my boots and a wind from the east lifts my skirts so they float like a sage green ghost around my thighs. The color of my clothing is drab, also Zegar's idea, to help me better blend into the surrounding woods. Tucked into the upper branches of a pine, I'm unlikely to be spotted by any of Agatha's men, should they somehow make it to Marwolaeth Island alive.

Unlikely, as the poisoned gasses within the dome that wreathe the island will kill any interlopers. That means Agatha's men can't come in and I can't get out—and that's the way it's been for a very long time. A stalemate. It's a stagnant middle ground I loathe. If it weren't for Zegar, I'd have taken my chances with the witch queen, Agatha, years ago. He knows it too and keeps an infuriatingly close eye on me as a result.

It must be spring in Neverland because the fog that hangs over the skyline has lightened from its usual sullen red to a lighter apricot shade. The sullied air is owing to the war machines they make in the Iron Coves—they belch black and red smoke into the sky, choking the life out of enemy and allies alike. The air isn't the only thing tainted—Agatha's people sap the magic from the ground, leaving barren rock in their wake. Perhaps she'll start tapping the ocean next, drying up the whole damn nation to create more land to squabble over.

It's no wonder the best and brightest fled Neverland long ago. Now there are only tales, echoes of their adventures to lend hope to the oppressed masses. Hope that there's a way out if you wish hard enough. Hard work, determination, and pixie dust. That's what got Peter, the Lost Boys, and Hook out of this gods forsaken place. I used to hope it would help me escape, too, but I gave up on ever escaping this place years ago.

I lean hard against the mast when I reach it. It's engraved with a million tiny characters, the glyph-based written language of the Seelie. I'm the only Seelie left. When Aunt Saxe shipped me here, she promised it was the only safe place to go.

That was ten years ago.

Aunt Saxe and I were the last of the Seelie and owing to the fact that Aunt Saxe is dead, that means I'm trapped on this island with no one but Zegar for company.

To Avernus with that.

It's not as if he's truly *bad* company. He's simply overbearing, more clucking mother hen than a crocodile shifter. Any hint of danger, and he's trying to smother me with cotton. He'll be angry I've come to the *Little White Bird* before sundown. *Too visible*, he'll say.

The ship beached itself on the shore of the island long before my arrival; the hull gouged out by the rocks. By the time I'd discovered it, it was little more than a skeleton. It was only my arduous work that restored it to its former glory. It's my hope that someday it will fly again.

The rustling of the nearby foliage is the only warning I get before Zegar comes crashing out of the woods and onto the black sand of the crescent-shaped beach. The waves that lap the shore are also dark, a heavy lead-gray from the oils the rest of the islands pump into them year after year. Barely anything lives in the water now. King Crab's men have to fish further and further offshore to find anything edible. The whales are all but gone; the population culled to collect fuel for Agatha's interminable fires.

I twist a little to face Zegar. He averts his eyes to preserve my modesty as the whipping winds continue to lift my skirts, giving him glimpses of my bare ass. It's not as if he hasn't seen it before, so I don't understand why he's clinging to propriety. There are only so many springs on the island in which to bathe. So, of course, we've come across each other nude before. Those moments are some of my more... enjoyable ones because Zegar's manhood is in a word—impressive. Not that anything has or ever will happen between us—I'm a tiny faerie and Zegar's half-giant. Size-wise, we just aren't a match.

Aside from Zegar's impressive nudity, it's not as if the rest of him isn't worth looking at. He's an intimidating ten feet tall, built broad and brawny, like any giant. He's a mixed breed—not altogether giant—and he favors his shifter mother, which means he's not as monstrously large as other giants. Still, when you're

4

four and a half feet tall as I am, almost everyone seems monstrously large.

Zegar's not wearing a shirt, and he's dripping wet. His sodden hair hangs in stringy lines around his face and shoulders, dipping to touch his mid-back. He must have cut his bathing time short when he found me gone. The view is enticing. I can't stop staring at him from where I stand high above him on the mainmast of my ship.

"Princess," he growls in that deep tone of his, which is now laced with anger. "Why do you insist on putting yourself in danger? I've told you a thousand times—"

"To keep my head down, so as not to attract Agatha's attention. I know, Zegar, because you're right—you have told me a thousand times!"

His thick green brows scrunch together, mashing lines into his face as he glares up at me. His brow ridge is more pronounced than human or even giant average. His brows are speckled with scales and give him a permanent menacing quality. He frightened me the first night he crawled onto the beach in his croc form, until he began clawing at his belly in clear agony. A crunching, grinding, clicking sounded from the bulge there. Long story short: I was forced to excise a clock from him and then nurse him back to health in my meager shelter. Now it's difficult to find someone, to whom you've played nursemaid, intimidating.

"Then why do you insist on defying me, Princess?"

I want to answer: that vexing him is one of the only

pastimes that interests me in my otherwise boring existence, but I'm too focused on another subject for the time being. "It's *Tinker*, Zegar. I swear you call me by that title just to vex me. But it's meaningless because we both know I rule over nothing. There's no one left *to* rule, even if I somehow make it back to Fantasia."

"Tinker sounds too..."

"Intimate?" I suggest and then smile as I narrow my eyes and jump down to the lower mast as he watches me and shakes his head, clearly unhappy. I do love making him uncomfortable. When I reach the lower mast, I sit down, my legs dangling over the side. His cheeks flush dark green with his irritation. There's a sandy brown cast to his skin. More evidence of his giant heritage. All the better to blend in with mud and moss.

I get up and stride down the plank, walking the precarious beam until I'm perched on the end. If I swan dive, will he catch me before I hit the ground? Hmm, it might be fun to find out.

"Princess, er, *Tinker*," he starts, clearing his throat and appearing completely uncomfortable as I continue to smile at him and even bat my lashes a few times. "Please come down from there."

"No, I won't." I cross my arms against my chest and give him my best stubborn expression.

His hands ball into fists at his side and frustration fairly leaks off him. "Be reasonable."

Oh, I do love upsetting him. There's nothing like a

frustrated giant—it's quite entertaining. "I am being reasonable," I answer with a shrug. "There not a blasted thing to do on this gods forsaken island, so you should allow my pleasure when and where I find it." I dance back and forth along the plank as he watches me with a mix of nervousness and irritation.

Zegar stares up at me for an uncomfortably long second. Then he says the only thing that can dissuade me from disobeying him.

"Return to camp and I'll tell you more tales of Pan and the Lost Boys."

I fight the urge to sit on the gangplank and kick my slippered feet furiously. My lip juts in a petulant pout, and I know I've been outmatched. I love tales of the Lost Boys. Zegar is far older than I, and remembers the Lost Boys before Agatha cursed him and them. He'd been tempted to join them on their voyage to Fantasia, but the crippling pain of the clock in his belly had kept him immobile for days. In the end, he'd been too late to join them.

What I wouldn't give to meet Peter Pan. I believe I'm half in love with him already. But if Pan and the Lost Boys found their solution to Agatha's curse on the other side of the waterfall, they're probably long dead. Still, I can dream of the boy with copper hair and an impish smile.

Pan occupies my thoughts more often than my dreams of killing my usurping Uncle Septimus and that's really saying something because the idea of destroying that bastard who ruined my life is one that visits me repeatedly. In fact, I have nightmares of Septimus weekly… he's never far from my mind. Thoughts of Septimus always spark the anger inside me and then I have to be careful to tame it back down again, because I know what happens if I'm overwhelmed…

I try to close my eyes against the memory, but it won't go away. It never goes away.

White light. Then incandescent blue. A shriek. The female shape shudders as the magic eats away at her own.

'Tinker stop!'

Her voice is breathless with pain. She claws at the cage of light. I stare, horrified, but am unable to stop it. The fear locks my limbs into place, and I stand useless as a statue as she burns.

"Come down here, Tinker," Zegar says quietly as the memory fades and I open my eyes, my heart pounding. The lines on his face have softened, as if he reads the ghost of that nightmare in my eyes. I've never told him the full story, but he's guessed enough—I can tell by the way he looks at me, like he's looking right through me.

"You promise you'll," I start but the wind steals my voice.

He nods. "I'll tell the story of Pan and the Lost Boys… yes, I promise."

It's hard to swallow. The sides of my throat stick together when I try. Still, I manage a weak smile.

"Thank you, Zegar."

8

I take a few running steps and fling myself into the open air. He catches me before I reach the ground, one large, muscled arm hooking around my waist, the other coming to rest beneath my back.

In the distance, I can hear the low-level moan of a detection charm going off. They're meant to mimic the call of a whale to throw off any invaders. I know better. If there are any whales still living, they won't be in the shallows near Marwolaeth Island.

My eyes lock with Zegar's. We both know what this means.

Something has finally breached the defenses.

"In the boat, Princess," Zegar orders, setting me on my feet. He reaches for his belt, shedding his trousers.

"Don't go," I whisper. "We both can hide aboard the *Little White Bird.*"

Even as I say the words, I know they'll do me no good. Zegar is a warrior. Warriors don't hide in ships while their charge is being attacked.

"Stay inside the ship and don't come out," he says warningly.

Then he's off, sprinting past the *Little White Bird,* feet slipping and sliding in the black sand until he disappears into the heaving surf, morphing into his crocodile shape. With little else to do, I climb aboard the ship again and slip below deck, confining myself to one of the servant's quarters, wishing I wasn't so useless. I ought to help Zegar. Instead, I cower here like a little dewdrop faerie, scared of my own shadow.

Incandescent blue. Shrieks. A plea for mercy.

9

I shudder, squeeze my eyes shut, and feel a single tear streak down my cheek. Zegar is right. I must stay inside.

My help will only get him killed.

TWO
PETER

"Put the feckin' bottle down, Peter. Ye're probably flammable at this point."

I glance askance at Quinn, who positions himself at the prow of our rickety little boat. It's barely larger than a canoe and about as suited to the turbulent waves. It's a modified version of the Piccadilly Tribe's favorite mode of transport. Wider to allow for more than two or three people at a time. Better balanced so a rower can stand at the aft and propel the craft forward with a long oar.

I lift the bottle and take another swig. After many years of drinking Sweetland Port or the picante Devil's Grot from Grimm, the stuff made in the Iron Coves tastes like troll piss. Reason one hundred and two why I prefer any principality in Fantasia to this shitty place.

I'll drink the piss-water anyway because it dampens the growing sense of dread I feel as we travel deeper into Neverland.

"Only if you flick a match at me," I counter. "Still got one in your hat, like your brother used to?"

Quinn's back stiffens and even in the low light from the lantern in the front row, I can see an angry flush creep up the back of his neck. He looks a lot like his brother, especially dressed as he is now, in a long-sleeved coat and a tricorn hat. The coat flaps in the icy winds coming off the waves.

His skin is darkly tanned from his time at sea, frozen that way forever after Agatha's spell ground our aging to a halt. His hair is much shorter than Hook's but precisely the same dark hue. He can pull it into a tail at the base of his neck. Quinn's the oldest of us and retains just a hint of stubble. The women think it's attractive. Not that he's been with a woman in the time I've known him—he hasn't. I've begun to think there's something wrong with him. Celibate for damn near forty years.

Insanity. I've more than made up for his lack, though.

"Dinnae ever compare my brother an' me again, Peter," Quinn says in his thick Scottish accent, spitting fire at me because I've forgotten the rule—don't mention his brother, the infamous Captain Hook. "Ah dinnae care if ye're shit-faced or nae. Ah'll still toss ye overboard."

Shame bubbles in my gut, making me abruptly nauseous. Or is that the liquor? Hard to say at this point.

I know better than to bring up Hook at a time like this. Quinn almost never speaks of him and we all respect that silence. Quinn had been in a sad state when I'd found him in Ironcross. He'd been reduced to nothing but skin and bones and he flinched like an abused dog every time one of the Generals in the King's army came near him. It wasn't hard to guess what they'd done to him. And that sort of thing wasn't uncommon—I'd been saving as many of the abused kids as I could. Not that Quinn had really been a kid. He's a year older than I am, but he'd needed saving, all the same.

That's how the Lost Boys came about. All of us abandoned, all of us mistreated, all of us orphaned. We're a family now. And no one fucks with the family.

I blow out a breath. "I'm sorry, Quinn. I should keep my damn mouth shut." I look around and glare at my surroundings. "It's just this place. I thought I'd die for good before I ever came back here."

"Me too," he whispers.

After arduous hours navigating the leaden waters, we've almost reached Marwolaeth Island. *Death Isle*, as it's more commonly known in the other Kingdoms in the archipelago. The poisonous vapors ensure no one gets in or out. The only reason we'll be able to get through the dome of vapors is owing to the vial of faerie dust we've been given by the Blue Faerie.

Legends say nothing, but wraiths and restless shades make their home on Marwolaeth. Except Tinkerbell.

The Blue Faerie says she's here. If Tinkerbell has survived, she'll be the only one in a hundred years who can say for certain what the isle is really like. And her surviving is a big *if*. Even Fae have to eat, and there's no telling if anything grows on Marwolaeth Island.

Maybe she died and her body was absorbed by the earth. I hear miraculous new places spawn from the death of Seelie Fae. It could be that we find a flourishing forest but no princess in sight. I hope not.

"It's time," Payne announces from the aft of our swaying vessel. He's been rowing the whole time, with no apparent fatigue.

I glance back at him with a frown. The Prince has been silent most of the journey, except to ask for course corrections. I've been trying to drown myself in a bottle, and Quinn has been nervously drumming his fingers on the side of the boat. We've all kept busy.

Quinn draws in a shaking breath. "Alright."

It's time to see if Saxe's magic still works, even after death. No reason it shouldn't, but still…

It would be just our luck that we meet our end here, in the vapors surrounding Death Isle. I always thought I'd die in Neverland because it would be quite an ironic death. It'll be a shame if that proves accurate.

Payne pauses his rowing just long enough to arrange us both on the floor of our rapidly shifting boat. The waves grow choppier the closer we get to that dense fog of poisonous gas. He rummages in his trouser pockets for a moment before producing two black pearls. Saxe says we're to suck on them, that they'll slow our heartbeat and breathing down to almost nothing, aping death as surely as the concoction that froze Briar Rose in place. Less permanent, thankfully. As our bodies will be essentially dead, we won't set an alarm to those dead who hover through the air. Payne scatters the vial of faerie dust around the boat, ensuring we make it through the dome. As we understand it, we'll wake as soon as we clear the vapors.

Payne won't need the spell, the lucky bastard. As a vampire, he's a corpse already. It will take more than a little poison to kill him for good.

I glare at the pearl in the palm of my hand.

"Saxe better be fucking right," I mutter.

Quinn turns his head to look at me, a slow grin spreading over his face. "Second star to the right."

"And straight on 'til morning," I finish. I can't help but grin a little at the shared joke. "Cheers, Quinn."

I toss the pearl up lazily and catch it on my tongue when it falls.

I'm out in seconds.

***

Salt water burns my nose as I come out of the spell... only to find myself drowning. The last time I can recall sucking in this much of the heaving surf, we were tracking Hook. Only the timely intervention of the Never Bird cut that short. My hands scythe the water, panicked as I choke on a lungful of the briny stuff.

Fuck! What's happened to our boat? Where are Payne and Quinn? Have we cleared the vapors around Marwolaeth Island? It's so dark, I can't see. Or is that just the stinging saltwater in my eyes? I swipe one hand quickly over my eyes and yes, that's part of the problem. Not far away I can see our capsized boat, bobbing along like a log, being carried further with each toss of the waves. I think I can see the flash of Payne's pale face a half-mile out, near a wall of thick, swirling vapor. So we have cleared the island's defenses, but only just.

I try to spin in place, but no matter which direction I look, I can't spy Quinn.

Fucking faerie spells. I won't lose one of my boys to this damn island. We all swore we wouldn't die in Neverland. I intend to keep that vow, even if I'm not sure I can. It's like this place calls to me—always has. I doubt I'll ever escape its smothering embrace.

There's a low, melancholic drone humming through the water. It sounds like a whale, but I doubt there's one in waters this shallow. They keep to the deeps, mostly, as King Crab's men have hunted them to near extinction.

There must be a second layer of protection we weren't warned about.

And just as I'm thinking as much, something sharp digs into my calf, just above my boot, driving in hot and deep like a dagger. I don't even have time to scream before I'm whipped beneath the waves and forced to hold my breath, lest my lungs fill.

Whatever has hold of me is large and strong, and it's pulling me down as quickly as it can. The pressure almost makes my ears pop, compresses my guts, and clenches me in a fist of cold so intense it boomerangs through me until it feels like I'm burning from the inside out. My mind conjures up a horrific image of a

16

mammoth shark that's got hold of my leg. The only thing that allows me to keep my head is the realization that if it were a shark, I'd be dead already. Sharks don't drown their victims intentionally—they hunt to feed. The creature beneath me isn't trying to eat me—it's trying to kill me.

I stuff my hand into the pocket of my long coat, praying to all that's merciful that I haven't lost the second vial of pixie dust the Blue Faerie gave us in preparation for the journey.

It's still there.

Thank the fucking Gods.

My fingers are numb with cold, so grasping the stopper that keeps the pixie dust in the waterproof wineskin Saxe stored it in isn't easy. The stuff is reserved for emergencies, but I think this qualifies. The cork finally comes loose, and I can feel the glittering motes slide between my fingers. The iridescent blue shines like a beacon in the deep. I reach up a hand to grasp it.

Faith, trust, and pixie dust.

That's all it takes to fly.

The light sinks into my palm and the power lights a fire in my gut that I long ago thought doused. I've tried, over the years, to bring such passion to the fore again, using sex, drink, and danger as substitutes. But, nothing compares to flying.

The last of my air bubbles out of me in a manic laugh as the pixie dust hauls me upward, toward the surface, dragging the creature attached to my ankle along with me.

Seconds later, I breach the waves, crowing as I spin into the open air. Just before the surface, the creature releases me. My calf still burns and the blood feels like the slop of molten rock against my skin as it bubbles from the deep punctures. But, I can't find it in myself to care. I feel lighter than air, free as a bird. It feels like I haven't taken a breath of fresh air in years. I'm reminded of the only reason I stayed in this damn place for so long.

Magic and flight.

I'm not completely fancy free, as the dome of vapors above Neverland does limit how high I can fly. But from this vantage point, I can make out our surroundings clearly. The worry that tied my guts into knots loosens when I see Quinn making his way toward the shore with sure strokes. Payne has managed to fight the waves to get back to the boat and is righting it.

Only I was attacked. Good.

The creature that attacked me snaps its teeth at me from below in mute frustration, poisonous yellow eyes glaring murder in my direction.

Familiar yellow eyes, I realize.

A grin curls my lips because I know the crocodile beneath me.

"Oi!" I shout down at the croc. "Zegar, you stupid bastard! It's me, Pan!"

For a moment, the crocodile makes no move to acknowledge me. Then, with a series of horrendous cracks and slurping sounds, the massive crocodile shifts into an only slightly less intimidating man.

I must have emerged nearer to shore than I thought, because he can stand without difficulty. He's in his half-giant form now. Ten feet tall, at least, and he's completely naked. Zegar easily has the largest appendage I've ever seen on a man—but I suppose it comes with the territory, since he is a half-giant. If he employs magic, he can access a full giant form. He almost never does.

Zegar parts stringy sheets of hair from his eyes and scowls up at me.

"What the fuck are you doing here, Pan?"

I smile down at him, pleased to see him, even if he's always been a sourpuss. And I have to admit—it is quite humorous to observe a stark naked and annoyed man. "How about a greeting or, failing that, an: '*I'm sorry I nearly just bit your leg off and drowned you, Pan*'?"

He glares right back at me. "What the fuck are you doing here, Pan?"

I want to counter with "What are *you* doing here, Zegar?" But I don't. Mocking him really isn't productive if we want to get out of Neverland alive and with Tinkerbell in hand. I hope Quinn still has the stone Maura gave him. Though at this point? It's a foregone conclusion.

Seelie extinguished, scales unbalanced, a lone light to guide the way. **She** *will depose the venal king and reforge the future of the fae.*

If she's still alive, Tinkerbell is the last living

19

Seelie Fae. She has to be the one the prophecy refers to. Still, it doesn't hurt to make sure.

I flash Zegar a cocky grin, fighting the urge to give another cock's crow. It'll be a shame to return to Fantasia, where I'm flat-footed and earthbound. Perhaps, with Tinkerbell in tow, I won't have to be limited to the ground. As her rescuer, surely, in return, she'd provide me with a pinch of pixie dust from time to time? If she's still alive, that is.

"I hear you've been hiding a Princess, Zegar. We've come to take her back."

Zegar squints at me uncertainly. "I don't know what you're talking about."

But, he does know—the truth is in his eyes—where it's located in all men.

"Come now, old chap," I start, shaking my head. "We've known one another far too long for falsehoods."

"It doesn't matter how long we've… been *acquainted*. I don't trust you."

My lip juts in a pout and my hand flies to my chest. "I'm wounded, Zegar! Shot in the heart! You've killed me!"

I fall down, stopping just shy of the waves, clutching my heart with a fist and making a choked sound of pain before flopping into the water on my back.

Zegar snorts a laugh, though there's frustration in the sound too. "Still absurdly dramatic, I see."

I crack one eye open so I can give him a scornful

look. "Absurdly dramatic? I am a noble thespian!"

"You're something alright," he grumbles. "A mercenary first and foremost, as I recall. Your first loyalty is to your crew and then to the pursuit of coin."

"All those things aside, I am here to rescue the princess."

"What princess?"

I frown and then shake my head. "Are we really going to play this game? I'm quite aware you are harboring the princess Tinkerbell in this accursed place. Thus, there is no reason to deny it."

Zegar is quiet for a few moments as he studies me with narrowed eyes. "How do I know her uncle hasn't bribed you into capturing and killing her?"

A huge breath of relief washes through me at the realization that Tinkerbell is still alive. And, more so, that Zegar knows where she is.

I lift the wineskin into the air so he can inspect it. It's only half full now, but the pixie dust is still fighting to get free of the container. Each mote is a slightly different shade of blue. Azure, teal, aquamarine, cerulean, indigo, cobalt—all dance and shift within the container. It tries to bubble out like sparkling ale overflowing a glass. I stopper the skin before the rest of the magic can escape. I'll need some of it later—to heal this wound Zegar's given me in my leg.

Zegar eyes the wineskin with extreme skepticism. "You could have taken that from the Blue Faerie's corpse."

He's closer to the truth than I'd like to admit. The

Blue Faerie *is* dead, just not... gone. She plans to lay herself to rest in the Anoka Desert when (I refuse to consider *if*) the war ends. Her body will be swallowed up then and the Anoka Desert will become some extraordinary place, not unlike the Enchanted Forest. Until then, the Blue Faerie is semi-animate and capable of giving magical advice and aid.

I shake the wineskin at him. "Do you think I could have gotten this before the ground swallowed her up? Use your brain, Zegar. I know it's a tiny thing battering around that cavernous skull of yours, but you *can* think."

Zegar takes a swipe at me and I roll clumsily to avoid him, taking in a glug of briny seawater before lifting off, cursing, and spluttering.

"Do you really think it's a good idea to insult me? I'm the only one who knows where the princess is."

"I'm sure I can find her if I search hard enough."

Zegar mumbles something under his breath, but doesn't take another swipe at me, which I find encouraging. Of course, that's when the bloodsucking pillock, Payne, decides to paddle over in the waterlogged boat. The werecrocodile turns his poisonous gaze on the newcomer and bares his teeth.

"Who's this?"

"Another member of my crew," I lie.

But, Zegar is too intelligent to fall for it. "Bollocks. He's too old and too dead." Zegar looks up at me. "You expected me not to disrespect you by lying to your face—extend me the same courtesy."

"Alright, I'm fibbing. He's not one of my Lost Boys, but he *is* a friend, Zegar. He's cursed, same as I am, just undergoing a different punishment."

Zegar looks at the vampire. "Who are you?"

"This is Prince Payne, and he rules one of the Kingdoms in Fantasia," I answer for Payne.

"Pleased to make your acquaintance," the vampire says to Zegar and continues his greeting with a practiced bow. The propriety is completely lost on Zegar, who is a brute through and through.

I wait for the information regarding Payne's lofty background to have some sort of impact on Zegar, then realize Payne's name will mean fuck all to him. I've spent decades on the other side, embroiled in the politics, the royalty and the courtiers. Zegar hasn't. He hasn't left this bloody isle. Thus, he won't know the infamous Payne and the blood thirst with which Payne was cursed by the Unseelie Fae, Maura LeChance. Zegar will only know what Tinkerbell knows, and that isn't much.

"Just take us to see her, please. We're planning to return her to Fantasia, where she belongs. It's long overdue."

That doesn't move Zegar. In fact, it seems to make him even more stubborn. His heavy, anvil-like jaw flexes, setting into an obstinate line. His eyes become chips of ice and he looks as if he might shift again.

"She's not ready."

I glare at him as I cross my arms against my chest. I'm tired of his recalcitrance—I've had quite the bumpy road in order to arrive at this hideous place, and while Zegar's obstinance was amusing at first, it's not any longer. "Ready or not, the spell is already breaking down since we passed the barriers. That means Marwolaeth Island isn't a safe haven for Tinkerbell any longer."

Zegar looks stricken. Then angry. And finally very, very tired.

"Damn you, Pan," he whispers, voice fervent and full of pain.

Unreasoning and uncharacteristic guilt twists in my stomach. I've managed to hurt my old ally, but I'm not sure how or why.

"I'll take care of her," I promise. "Lay down my life for her if such is necessary."

The ice in his stare doesn't thaw. "You'd better, Pan. Because if something befalls her, I'll come after you, myself."

THREE
TINKER

Someone is coming.

Maybe multiple someones.

I can hear the heavy footfalls coming through the woods, snapping twigs, and rustling the pine needles that lay like a thick, prickly carpet on the paths that wind through the island.

I curl a little further in on myself, clutching my knees to my chest, my head laid on top of them, curling my wings forward so they cover most of me.

My shoulders hunch even further forward. I will probably have to call on my magic—something I try to reserve for emergencies. The last time I used magic in fear or anger...

White light. Then incandescent blue. A shriek.

Shudders ease down from my shoulders all the way down to my slippered feet, and I know I can't call on my magic. Even though doing so may be the only thing that can save my life, I can't. No one else should die in agony the way *she* did.

It's been years, but I still recognize the heavy tread of a Neverland mercenary's boot. When my Aunt Saxe spirited me away to Neverland for my safety, we were forced to navigate dangerous waters and fight for our lives against the savage armies of several Neverland factions.

They all wear armor and heavy boots. No such thing as a civilian in Neverland. You armor up from the time you're able to walk, then you fight a fruitless war until you're killed by disease or the enemy.

Speaking of the enemy, I wonder which monster Agatha and Septimus have sent to kill me? One of their foot soldiers, the batmen? They're grotesquely misshapen, made so by Agatha's dark magic. Bat-like faces and wings, with the lower body of a wolf, so they almost appear to be wearing hairy trousers. They're driven mad for blood and are just as likely to kill their enemies as they are to bring them in alive.

Zegar has told me many stories about the batmen and how they used to be regular folk—citizens of places like Sweetland, before Agatha and her dark magic perverted them into the dark abominations they are today. As Zegar tells it, Agatha and my uncle forced the physician of Sweetland to create a magical venom to which Agatha added her dark magic. That venom was distributed to the townspeople and, thus, Agatha's and Septimus' legion of batmen was born. They didn't just create the batmen either, they also created hellhounds and other monstrous abominations.

I think I prefer the batmen to the Priapens though. The batmen are made as I said, not born and thus don't have any genitals or sexual desire. The Priapens are what the Fantasian people call incubi and succubae.

They are cunning, beautiful, and strong. Probably not strong enough to bypass Zegar if he's standing in their way. At least, not in regular combat. But, if one of the Priapen women had him pinned beneath her on the shore, he would be mating her with wild abandon with no thought of me, or anything else, for that matter.

That thought clenches my stomach in a vice grip of jealousy. It's irrational, but in the last few years I've begun to think of Zegar as mine, even though he isn't. He's the only friend I've got in this hideous place and I won't lose him to some sexual demoness. I won't.

And I won't lose myself to a sexual demon, either. I don't want my first sexual experience to be a Priapen raping me to my death, even though that would perhaps be better than being torn apart by the batmen.

The heavy footsteps stop just outside my hiding place, and a gentle voice calls my name.

"Tinker, it's alright. You can come out now."

The voice is familiar—Zegar's—and instantly calms my nerves. Tears of profound relief sting my eyes.

I spring lightly to my feet and then I'm a blur of wings, zipping out the door. I'm just—so happy to hear his voice! Hang the consequences of spreading my pixie dust everywhere! I need to make sure he's alright, throw my arms around him and squeeze him as tightly as I can. In seconds, I've cleared the corridor, the stairs and am floating lightly above the deck. I alight on the rail once more so I can beam down at Zegar. I want to swan dive off the side again, land in his arms, and hug him senseless.

I don't, though, because Zegar isn't alone.

Three other men stand just behind him and off to the side, staying in his periphery, seemingly mindful that Zegar needs to be aware of their position to maintain a sense of calm. Zegar is uncomfortable letting me go off on my own to find food. I can't imagine the level of anxiety he must feel with three Neverland soldiers within shooting distance of me. None appear to have a range weapon on their persons, but if they're fast enough or skilled enough with arcane magic, they could still harm me.

Zegar is remarkably calm, and I can't puzzle out why. Maybe it's because all three men are much smaller and slighter than he? One of them seems especially waifish, too fragile to be a mercenary. He seems the sort to be mowed down in the first wave of combat.

But... no. There's something about him...

Confidence, maybe even arrogance, exudes from every pore of his pale skin. I can see it in the blue-green eyes that peek out from beneath his hat and his fringe of copper hair. He stands straight and almost regal in his green body armor. With a jolt of surprise, I realize the armor is Fae-made. Genuine Seelie craftsmanship of the sort that hasn't existed since before the war with Morningstar. Who could have made it for him? And how has he kept it? It must be the envy of every soldier in Neverland.

When he moves, he does so with a limp. I look

down and realize he's wounded—there's blood staining his pants just below his left knee. There's a leaf-edged sword hanging at his waist, also faerie made. If used to defend the innocent, it will always find its mark and cut true. The Seelie were a peaceful people and we don't thirst for blood or vengeance the way the Unseelie do. Our weapons are always defensive. The dagger strapped beside the sword must be the one he uses offensively.

His companion on his left side is slightly taller, though if he's older, I would be surprised. This young man is also wearing body armor beneath a frock coat, though his is made of mundane leather. His skin is bronzed from his time in the sun and he hangs behind the arrogant one like a shadow. His hair is dark, softly waving and pulled into a tail at the base of his neck, the majority of it hidden by a pirate's hat. I have the odd urge to run my fingers through it to see if it's as soft as it appears.

He glances up at me from under thick lashes. When our eyes meet, he stares and his cheeks flush a ruddy hue. A shy mercenary? That's something I've never heard of before.

And the third in their group is an undead. I can feel the death magic reverberating around him, and it makes me uneasy.

"Who are you?" I ask the copper-haired one finally. Zegar doesn't appear keen on making introductions, and we can't stare blankly at each other forever.

He smiles—wide and puckish. There's a twinkle of mischief in his eyes that's so infectious I want to laugh. I have the impression he's just as likely to say something outlandish as he is to give a proper introduction. He whips the hat off with a flourish and bows at the waist.

"The name's Peter, m'lady. Though most of my boys call me Pan."

Peter Pan! My mouth pops open wide enough I could swallow dewdrop faeries whole. Pan? As in *the* Peter Pan? The scourge of pirates? The mercenary leader who has led more successful missions than any other man in history? The Pan that lopped off Hook's hand and fed it to Zegar? *That* Peter Pan?

I feel my stomach drop all the way down to my toes as Peter continues to introduce the others. "This somber bloke behind me is my second, Quinn Teach, though he doesn't like the last name much, so just Quinn, if you don't mind."

And Quinn!

Zegar tells tales of him, as well. Not good with a sword or on a ship, but Quinn's a crack shot with any range weapon. Slingshot, arrows, chakkar, throwing knives. He's strong and accurate for over a mile. Eyes like a falcon's and speed that beggars belief. Next to Pan, he's the most competent killer in Neverland.

Peter Pan and Quinn!

They're standing right in front of me.

"And this is Prince Payne," Peter finishes as the undead takes a step forward and bows gallantly. I narrow my eyes at him—as a general rule, I don't trust the undead. Yet, I'm too focused on the fact that Peter Pan and Quinn are standing before me to even bother about the vampire prince.

I can't believe it. Is this a dream? And if it is, why did Zegar bring them here without at least giving me a forewarning? I mean—I'm so underdressed! A stiff breeze will hike my skirt and reveal I'm not wearing small clothes. Though I fancy myself half-in-love with Peter already, that doesn't mean I want him to see my nether bits… well, *yet*, anyway!

I fist my hands in my skirt self-consciously, ready to bat it down in the case of a sudden gale. I sway a little on the rail. Good Gods! This is really happening. They're here! I don't know how or why, but it's as plain as the nose on my face.

"T-Tinker," I manage to stammer out.

"Excuse me?" Peter asks.

"My… name… my name is Tinker," I explain, feeling a blush stealing across my cheeks. My throat is dry and it's difficult to swallow. I feel like a little sprite again. Peter is only two feet taller than me at most, but in my mind he's as much a giant as Zegar. I almost feel unworthy to be in his presence.

Peter's grin could light a room. Those eager eyes take me in and, to my shock, don't seem to find me lacking.

"A pleasure to meet you, Miss Tinker. May I call you… Tink?"

"Y-yes!"

He can call me whatever he likes, so long as he keeps looking at me like that. I like the way he looks at me—it's an expression that seems somehow familiar, like we're old friends who haven't seen one another in a long while. I want to be his friend. Oh, that's not true! I want to be far more than friends!

But, baby steps, Tinker, baby steps!

"Well Tink, Quinn, Payne and I are here on behalf of your aunt."

"You are?" I ask, the news swelling my heart, before I realize it's impossible. "But, she's—"

Peter clears his throat, interrupting me, and gives me a half nod before he quickly changes the subject. "It's time to take you back home, to Fantasia."

"At this very moment?" I ask, suddenly thinking I'm not prepared. Of course, I don't have much to pack, really. But, my ship... I look up at it and feel a mote of sadness overcome me.

"Well, not at this very moment," Peter corrects himself. "Our friend, Prince Payne, has to sleep for the coming of the day, but once evening is upon us, we'll be off. Presuming such is okay with your highness?"

Yes. A million times yes.

I'm choking on my own joy at the thought of leaving Neverland far behind me. Even if that means leaving my ship... it's an offer I can't refuse. There are no words to express how happy I am in this moment. Not only has someone come to rescue me from this wretched place, but that someone is *him*. Would it be too forward to invite him to my quarters for the

32

evening? I want to show him my appreciation. Preferably more than once.

"Thank you," is all I can manage.

Then I zip back below deck, leaving a trail of pixie dust in my wake, before I can burst into joyful tears in front of the only man I've ever idolized.

My childhood God.

My Peter Pan.

FOUR
QUINN

I don't want to heave my last meal onto the floor of the princess' ship. She's clearly very proud of it, smiling shyly at Peter and me as she gives us a thorough tour of what she built, when she built it, and what spells imbue the wood. I notice with some amusement that she doesn't bother even looking at Payne, much less talking to him. Not that he seems to mind—he's a strange one, but given his undead nature, I suppose that's a given.

But, back to the ship: it's impressive. *She's* impressive. But I still want to be sick.

Why didn't I take Peter's out when he offered it? None of the Lost Boys wanted to come back here, but I've arguably suffered the most. Neverland has repeatedly fucked me in the ass—literally. Riddle or Mayhaps volunteered to accompany Peter and I should have let them, owing to the fact that I absolutely detest this place. So why didn't I?

Because Peter and I are the oldest and the strongest, that's why. We're the most capable the Lost Boys have to offer and the Seelie Princess is too valuable to lose. She's Chosen and if we can reunite her with the other Chosen, that will mean we have six of the ten. The Guild's morale has never been higher. It seems like soon we'll have the firepower necessary to face down the Great Evil.

And just in time, too.

The seals are gone, the monsters out and wreaking havoc all across Fantasia. Vita has traveled from village to village, draining every last person of their vitality. There are so many dead, the Shepherds are struggling to keep up if they're able to access the dead at all. Lycaon is summoning hellhounds by the thousands, Bacchus has reformed his revelry and bespelled the north half of Grimm. Delorood, Ascor, and Sweetland are bearing the brunt of the attacks, taking a great deal of punishment for having the gall to side with the Guild.

We need her. We need Tinker.

So why am I having a difficult time not resenting her?

Of course, I know the answer as soon as I've asked the question. Because, in my heart and mind, I've never truly left Neverland. Or maybe it's more accurate to say *it's* never left me. The fucking curse my brother saddled us with after fucking and then spurning Agatha means I'm stuck forever at nineteen, unable to move forward, no matter how hard I try. I'm always an abused wretch, abandoned by his brother, abused by his captors, and cursed for an act I didn't commit.

Tinker seems sweet, but I feel animosity towards her, regardless.

35

And she's fucking beautiful, but that doesn't matter. Because women are all the same—they flock to Pan no matter what. I'm sure the second they have the privacy, she'll be riding Peter's cock—just the same as all the others. Already, she's developed a sort of puppyish hero worship where he's concerned, asking questions about our many exploits over the years. Peter's never been finicky when it comes to bed partners, taking plain farm girls to his bed just as easily as a comely barmaid.

Bedding Tinker will be novel for him. In all his years, he's never bedded a Fae. Too damn dangerous to try with the Unseelie, even for a dicer like Peter, and the Seelie were long gone by the time he had the inclination.

But, back to Tinker—she's just so damn naïve. Her innocence fairly screams from her and I can't help but feel she deserves better than being just another of Peter's curiosity fucks. Regardless, I don't see a way to stop it at this point, shy of having Zegar twist Peter's head off like a cork. While it would be the sort of ending Peter deserved after breaking so many hearts, it won't keep the princess safe from his devilish ways.

Ye could always take her to yer bed, my brain traitorously supplies.

My stomach heaves again, and I brace my hand on the wall. It thrums with faerie power. No. I can't. Not without thinking of Mistress Chamir. And the chains. The degradation as she and her husband...

No. I can't.

I must have made a sound because Tinker stops in the middle of the hall, half-turning toward me. Her thin brows mash together over her eyes. They're so large and luminous. I've almost forgotten the look of huge, Seelie eyes. She's exceptionally beautiful, even among the Fae I've had the privilege to know. Tanned skin, eyes the color of a cloudless summer sky, thick, lustrous mahogany curls that can't quite cover the points of her ears.

The facial markings are an upraised, intricate ivy pattern. I've had the urge to run my thumbs over them since I clapped eyes on her. But, she's been busily tending to Peter's wounded leg, sprinkling it with the fairy dust given to us by Saxe and then bandaging it up tight with some native leaves. I'm not sure why she doesn't just use her own fairy dust, but I don't question her.

"Quinn?" My name comes out a timid question. "Are you alright?"

I struggle to find something to say that won't offend her. "Ah… Ah think Ah should step ootside. The journey here didnae agree with me."

Did that sound diplomatic enough? I hope so, because I'm almost past the point of caring. I need to be outside, away from the confining sleeping quarters she's led us into. This ship reminds me too much of the Jolly Roger, and that fateful day my brother allowed me to be sold into slavery.

I'd at least shucked off the name I'd earned. Neverland is all about the name you're given, not the

37

one you're born with. Back then, they'd called me 'Barnacle'. Something ugly and unwelcome on a ship. I was and always will be Quinn now.

Before she can say anything else, I turn to stride back up the corridor, take the steps up to the deck two at a time until I can reach fresh air. Yes, it's still stale and sooty from the endless fires and steam machines that churn every day and night. But Gods, it's something, at least. I can breathe a little easier. There's a reason I sleep on the roof of every inn we frequent. Easier to get away.

The stars are shining bright.

It might be peaceful to climb a tree and find a branch on which to settle in for the night. I need to rest if I'm to take on Agatha's men on the return trip. I saw many during the voyage here. Hairy batmen. The swaggering, inhumanly beautiful Priapen. I've been had by a few of those too. Their beauty is skin deep, as false as a whore's smile. Once their magic loses its potency, they smell like fetid meat and their skin chafes like sandpaper.

I'm absorbed in studying the landscape; deciding whether a tree or the shallow trench that had probably once been a creek is more easily defensible. It's probably why I don't hear her approach until her fingers softly skim my elbow. A shout flies from my mouth, echoes into the night, and I jerk away so hard I hit the railing. Even before I've turned to see her response, I already know mine is an overreaction. It's just this damned place.

Tinker stands just behind me, one small, dainty hand extended toward me helplessly while a small fish hangs from a line on the other.

"I... thought you might like supper," she mumbles sheepishly. Her cheeks flame with color and her eyes drop immediately to the deck.

Gods, I'm being a bastard. She's clearly starved for attention and approval. Strong and capable Zegar may be, but 'warm' isn't a word I'd apply to him. He can't help it. Crocodiles run cold and aren't very paternal. Not only that, but giants are aggressive so poor Zegar is battling both emotional fronts—there's not a warm bone in his body. And, yet... I saw the way he looked at the princess. I saw the way true caring alighted in his eyes. Aye, he loves her alright, but it doesn't appear he loves her in a sexual way. How that's possible, I'm not sure. Not only does she have a comely face, but her body is just as comely—shapely and curvaceous, just as a woman's should be. And she's barely clothed. As she moves, we all got glimpses of her tight, little rear and her pert and small breasts were on display as she bent over, more than once.

"Ah'm nae very hungry," I mumble.

I can't quite meet her eyes. Concern leaks off her, so warm and sincere, it makes my heart ache. When was the last time a lass cared a whit about me?

Goldy? Aye, perhaps, but she's like a sister to me. I could no more bed her than I could my dearly departed mum. And Goldy feels the same way. She never looked at me the way Tinker looks at me now.

Her huge eyes glimmer wetly in the starlight, and my stomach pitches again, this time in guilt.

"Did I... did I do something wrong, Q-Quinn? Or did I say something wrong? Because if I offended you, I'm s-sorry." She drops her gaze and makes arching shapes in the sand with her toes. "I don't know how to talk to men. Especially not men like you. All I've had is Zegar for company and as I'm sure you know, he's not really a scintillating conversationalist. If you want, I can…"

I'm not sure what possesses me in that instant. I'm not like my brother or Peter—I don't have a way with women. I don't chase and I don't charm them for my own ends. In general, I avoid them. But I know it's my fault the princess is standing here so awkwardly and apologizing for something she has no business apologizing for.

Before I can think, before I can stop myself, my hands are suddenly cupping the sides of her tiny, breakable face. I'm able to cradle it all and then some. She's so incredibly small. Her skin is warm beneath my splayed fingers. Her breath hitches, confused and excited, and her eyes are wide with shock, just before I slant my mouth over hers.

Her mouth is soft and warm, though it almost feels too small. Mistress Chamir had a broad mouth, and it felt like she was trying to swallow me whole whenever she kissed me. I shudder, trying to push the memory away. This isn't Mistress Chamir. This is Tinker. The delicate Fae woman who's so incredibly fragile in this

40

moment, it feels like one wrong move or word will break her.

My hands weave their way into her curls and tug a little at the nape of her neck. Yes. Not Mistress Chamir. Her hair was long, golden, and a little lank from lack of washing. It would often be matted with blood or filth from the battleground. She liked to fuck when she came home from a successful conquest. Tinker's dark curls are an anchor, a reminder that I'm not there. I'm not a victim any longer. I am Quinn, decider of my own destiny.

Her lips part, and a gentle sigh eases out of her. Her wings blur into motion, showering us both with golden-green dust. Her hands come up to grip my biceps through the coat and then both our feet lift from the ground.

Flying.

Peter will be green with envy. He's never kissed a Fae princess in mid-air before, and I've beaten him to it. Not my intent, but still... it's very nice.

The kiss seems simultaneously too brief and to stretch toward infinity. It's a magic moment, locked in place. I know I won't forget it. And strangely? Her touch doesn't scare me half-out of my mind. Perhaps it's because she's so different from any other woman I've kissed.

Perhaps it's magic? I doubt I'll ever know for certain.

"Ah'm sorry," I whisper, pulling back, at last. "Ah didnae mean to take liberties with ye, yer grace."

41

"No," she insists, her cheeks flushed and her eyes just as wide. She looks up at me with the same expression she gave Peter earlier—one of adoration.

"Yer ship is a marvel o' Fae craftsmanship; Ah jist dinnae care for small spaces."

Or ships. Or this fucking place. Anything that reminds me of the past I thought I'd left far behind. Not that I can tell her that. I don't want her to know just how broken I am. I want her to continue looking at me just like she is.

Tinker's entire face brightens. "Then I haven't done something to upset you?"

"Nae!" I insist. "Ah jist… it's as Ah explained."

She nods. "I think I can help you... I have a place I go when I need to get away from Zegar to be alone with… just my thoughts. It's perfectly safe, if you'd like to sleep there instead?"

I'm so relieved, I want to kiss her again. "That would be much appreciated, yer grace."

"Tink," she corrects. "Please call me Tink. I rather… like the name."

"Because Peter gave it to ye?" I don't mean for my tone to sound so… pointed, but there it is.

Her cheeks flush, and she chews her lip. "Perhaps, but I also like the informality of it. Zegar can be such—"

"A humorless bastard?"

She smiles but shakes her head. "He means well."

"Aye, but it doesnae change the fact he's got to be as excitin' to live with as a corpse… nae offense to

42

Prince Payne."

"Not a corpse, precisely," she starts.

I offer her a tiny smile to soften the words. "Sorry. Mayhap that's a bit o' an overstatement. Why dinnae ye show me this place o' yours, before Ah manage to choke on me own boot leather?"

Her laugh is a whispering thing, like the path the wind takes through the trees. Strangely, it calms my nerves. If I close my eyes, I can almost pretend I'm camped in the Enchanted Forest, feeling the lull of the forest.

Tinker slides her tiny hand into mine. Again, she feels too small, like a child is gripping my palm instead of a full-grown Seelie Princess. I glance down at her curiously, one eyebrow cocked.

"Whit are ye doin'?" I don't like it when anyone touches me… usually.

"It's faster if we fly," she explains. "Low, of course, so we don't attract attention. Zegar would drop an egg or two on the spot if he knew I was zipping above the treetops."

My smile comes easier this time, and there's a note of laughter in my voice when I speak. "Ye do know Zegar's a male, right?"

She giggles and the sound is like bells ringing. "Of course I do, silly. That's why it will be so impressive when he does it."

I squeeze her hand tight, grateful to her for this unexpected kindness. Her presence is like a bolstering shot of Devil's Grot. It settles in my belly like fire.

"Alright then, Tink. Let's fly."

FIVE
TINKER

Fae bodies can be deceptive, because we're so small. Zegar says I can be mistaken for a child from a distance if one doesn't pay too much attention to my chest. And not paying attention to my chest is, admittedly, easier to do than I might like. I never inherited my mother's generous proportions. But I'm a full-grown Seelie Fae and that means I have *at least* the physical prowess of the average carnival strongman locked into a delicate frame.

Maybe Quinn thinks me weak, because he lets out a yelp of surprise when I use my grip on his hand to swing him into my arms in what Aunt Saxe once called a 'princess carry'. He's awkward to carry, as he's so much larger than I am, but I can manage, all the same. Almost the entire length of his legs dangle off my arms, and the rest of him towers over me as he tries to right himself.

"Don't squirm," I warn him.

My wings blur into motion and we're off, shooting through the trees, leaving golden-green sparks in our wake. The sparks fall to earth in a soft golden shower and, occasionally, a flower pops up from the ground as soon as the spark lands. My body thrums in time with my sprinting heart, pulsing joy through me like sweet, heady wine.

I'm no longer alone on this island and the thought is sweet like honey. Though... *technically* I was never alone—because I had Zegar for company—it still felt like I was because Zegar isn't really a social type. Furthermore, he usually only joins me for mealtimes and his conversation is stilted and sullen. Zegar is a recluse. Sometimes I almost think it might have been easier if he hadn't been on the island with me; it's worse to feel alone when in the company of someone else than it is to feel alone all by yourself. As I've grown, I've become more curious about the ways of the world (and, specifically, the ways of men) and damn proper as he is, Zegar won't indulge me in any of my... carnal pursuits.

Will Quinn? Hmm, I'm not sure. Yes, he kissed me, but there's something closed off about Quinn—like one of those mysteries you never have a hope of finding out. I have a feeling Peter would indulge me if I asked him. What more could I hope for than to lose my maidenhead to *the* Peter Pan?

Still... there's something about Quinn. The tenderness of his touch, the sweetness of his kiss, that look in his eyes—I can see how this man would be addicting. And that tinge of sadness in his eyes—it makes me want to understand what has upset him, why he carries a cloud of sorrow. I want to chase his sadness away. He's too good a man to wrestle such phantoms.

"Feck," Quinn breathes as the forest floor becomes a mottled green-brown blur beneath us. The trees are dense here and I have to zig-zag to avoid colliding with anything. We're nearly there. I hope the speed isn't making him sick.

"Are you alright?"

"Ah'm fine… it's jist..." he swallows audibly. "'Tis me first time flyin'."

That slows me just a little. Dangerous to pause mid-flight the way I want to—I'm not especially good at hovering. His statement confuses me, though.

"All the Lost Boys fly in the stories, I thought?"

Quinn barks a humorless laugh. "Ha! Our glorious tales o' victory. Most o' those stories are naethin' but cods wallop."

I'm still confused and, admittedly, a little disappointed. "So... you don't fly?"

"Peter does when he's got access to pixie doost. Used to have a Faerie godmother 'fore the siege of Ironcross. But, she was killed durin' the sack o' the city. Ah expect Peter will ask ye for pixie dust afore we leave for Fantasia. He'll fly with ye happily."

"Oh." I'm suddenly worried I've upset him. The edge of bitterness is creeping back into his voice, his eyes going distant and hard again. His jaw, lined with attractive stubble, sets. "Do you want me to put you back down?" I ask quietly. I wonder if he'll hear me through the wind whipping around our ears.

He cranes his neck to look at me, those kind eyes softening. "Nae. Ignore meh. Ah'm jist a cranky old man."

I scoff. "You're not an old man."

He chuckles and it's a deep, melodious sound. "Ah'm fifty-nine, lass. Ah havenae aged since Agatha's curse was cast."

"And I'm sixty-five, so there," I say, sticking my tongue out at him playfully.

He blinks. "Yer fibbin'. Ye dinnae look it at all."

I shrug. "Fae stop aging at physical maturity. And for the record, I'm still a child by the standards of the others. Sixty-five is a drop in the bucket when your lifespan is potentially infinite."

Quinn thinks about that and then laughs again. I do love the sound. "Damn. Ah hadnae really considered that. Ye look good, lass."

We emerge from the trees and zip into my refuge, the place I spend my time if I'm not repairing the *Little White Bird*.

Feeling playful, I let Quinn go without warning, knowing his landing will be soft. To my surprise, he doesn't fall on his rear, instead twisting like a cat in mid-air to land solidly on his feet. His boots impact the soft earth and he slides a few inches before regaining his balance. He cuts a striking figure, silhouetted against the moon. The vapors that have always wreathed the island are rapidly dissipating. Now that they've been breached, the island is no longer safe. Strangely though, I feel safe with Quinn. I almost feel as if I know him from all the stories Zegar has told me about him and the other Lost Boys. I have this feeling

Quinn won't allow me to be harmed.

"'Tis beautiful," he breathes, staring out at the blue lagoon.

I smile so hard, my cheeks hurt. I've always thought this place was beautiful too, but I've never gotten confirmation of that fact from someone else. I've been too scared to allow Zegar here, knowing he'll react badly to the means by which I created it.

The trees that ring my lagoon have waxy trunks and broad, green leaves. They belong in a desert oasis, not this little pine-riddled island. The lagoon's water shines brilliant blue, sparkling waves hitting the shore every few seconds. It's a brighter blue than anything I've ever seen, save my Aunt Saxe.

White light. Then incandescent blue. A shriek.

The joy drains away rapidly, like water being let out through a drain. I don't deserve happiness. Not a second of it. Not after what I've done. I swallow hard, and I hate the weighty feeling in my stomach. No matter what I do, where I go or how I hope to feel happiness, I can never escape my past. It haunts me and always will.

"Ah've never see anythin' like this," Quinn says slowly, turning to take in the full view. "Ah had nae idea these trees grew in Neverland. Ah've never seen anythin' but pine or oak before. Most islands have been largely deforested anyway, so 'tis nae as though Ah've seen a lot..."

"They don't grow here. *I* made them grow."

Quinn half-turns to me, frown lines appearing

between his brows and around his mouth. Only in that instant does he truly look his age.

"Whit do ye mean?"

I kick at the dirt with the toe of one slipper. Will he shout at me, like Zegar would if he found out? Based on his temperament, Peter will probably agree with me that my little oasis was a worthwhile sacrifice but...

"Seelie corpses make forests, gardens, or beautiful landscapes," I begin slowly, unable to meet his eyes. "It began as an accident... and then... I kept... *experimenting*."

"Tinker," he says warningly, as he narrows his eyes at me. "Whit did ye do?"

Yes, he's definitely as bad as Zegar. I ought to stop talking, but now if I stay silent, he'll assume the worst.

"When Zegar washed ashore, he was mostly dead. That's how he managed to fool the security system of this island. When I was digging in his guts, trying to remove that clock, he was thrashing this way and that and I ended up cutting myself on a piece of the clock and my blood leaked into the sand and it... sort of spawned a section of the lagoon. So I kept coming back to... add to it."

"Ye're mutilatin' yerself to create a paradise?"

I'm taken aback by the anger on his face. "Hardly mutilating myself! It's just a little cut here or there."

"Ye shouldnae intentionally hurt yerself for any reason. Dinnae ye know what ye're worth? Who ye are? Whit ye mean to the rest o' the world?"

My wings blur into motion, lifting me from the

ground, sending up a cloud of glittering dust. It settles into his dark hair and twinkles like stars in the night. When he blinks up at me, I note how my dust has also settled onto his lashes. They're quite long and brush his skin when he blinks. It's almost unfair how attractive he is. It makes it difficult to hold my irritation to my chest, but that anger continues to burn me like an ember, stoked by his presumption.

"My worth?" I laugh at him.

He nods, expression uncorrupted. "Aye."

"And what worth is that?"

"Ye are… special, Tinker. Surely, ye moost know what ye are?"

"I'm so special that my aunt left me here to rot!" I whirl around myself, taking in my surroundings. "I've been nothing but a prisoner here, stuck on this damned island for as long as I can remember. That doesn't sound very special to me."

"Ye are. Ye are one o' the," he starts, but I interrupt as I turn around to fully glare at him.

"Do you know how lonely it was before Zegar? I had nothing and no one! If he hadn't washed ashore, I'd be half-mad by now."

"Neither of ye could have known yer aunt would perish, Tink," he says, voice conciliatory. His anger isn't a lasting thing, like mine. It sizzles, hot like water on a heated iron and then evaporates. I can see why he's a good compliment to Peter. The stories say Pan is as spiteful as he is impetuous.

"Ah'm sure she didnae mean ye to be alone," he

finishes in a softer voice.

I *did* know she'd perished. Because I'd been the one to kill her…

The thought weighs heavily on my shoulders, the hot flash of shame spreading across my chest until my skin glows a sickly green from it. I jerk in midair when Quinn reaches up to stroke his index finger from my bare knee down to my ankle. Faeries find it difficult to grow hair, so I'm bare almost everywhere, but my head and brow.

His touch doesn't feel sexual, but with the blood burning hot beneath my skin, any touch feels intimate. And I suddenly need to focus on something else—to escape the memories that continue to haunt me, never allowing me far from their grasp. So I focus on the rough texture of his hands and the way they make me shiver. I want to feel his hands in other, more private places. What would it feel like for that rough hand to cup my mound, my breasts?

A shiver runs from my toes all the way up to the points of my ears. Faeries are nature's creatures. Sex is in my nature, though I haven't had intercourse yet. Everything leading up to it but...

"Whit happened?" Quinn asks, mild curiosity in his tone. "Ye turned green all o' a soodden."

"Nothing," I say, hurriedly changing the subject. I can't think about my past, what I've done. I hate myself for it.

And I can't bear the thought of telling him the truth. Even Zegar doesn't know for certain what happened, what the truth is. He guesses, but he's never asked outright. What if they learned the truth and then they packed up and left without me? What if the truth disgusts even Zegar and he turns his back on me, as well? Would they leave me alone on the island? Or worse, would they kill me? Death is still the penalty for murder in Fantasia, isn't it?

"Yer skin is so smooth..." Quinn says under his breath. He grasps my calf, and I can feel the sturdy strength of his hands. Every nerve ending I have sings at the contact. I've been alone for so long...

I dip down toward the ground, sliding his hand from my calf, over my knee and coming to rest on my thigh. His fingers brush the soft swell of my thigh, dip into the vee just before my sex.

"I'm smooth… *bare* all over," I say, trying for my best sultry purr. I've not had much practice, so it comes out a little uncertain. "You could touch me, if you like."

Quinn jerks his hand back quickly, as though my flesh burns him. His eyes go distant, a little glassy, and panic almost radiates from his skin. Fae are sensitive, and so I can taste his fear on my tongue. It's sour, like the taste of bile.

I flush once again, this time in embarrassment. How stupid of me, propositioning one of the Lost Boys. Of course he doesn't want me. I'm not even his species! He has to have a bevy of human women eager to warm his bed each night. He doesn't need a murdering Seelie princess.

Shame and mortification take turns nearly choking

me. "I..." My voice barely comes out. My eyes are burning with the effort it takes not to cry. I need to get out of here before the tears spill over. I'm mortified enough. I don't need to devolve into hysterics in front of my heroes. "I'll leave you to sleep. There's a bower a little way up the path. The mosses and flowers can make for a comfortable bed. I've hidden from Zegar there a time or two."

My wings blur into motion again and I've zipped a few yards back the way I'd come, when a hand closes around my forearm and yanks me to a stop. It's so startling, I jerk forward in midair, my heart riding up into my throat. I whirl around to face my captor and find Quinn floating just behind me, listing this way and that like he's on a shaking balance beam. Unsurprising, given we're ten feet off the ground. I believe him when he says he's never flown before. He clearly hasn't found his sea legs yet. Or rather, his *sky* legs. He's more uncertain than a newborn sprite.

"Dinnae leave," he says, drawing me to him. He anchors himself with my shoulders, seeming steadier when he holds me. Then he draws me close enough to hear his heart pounding against his ribs. "Dinnae fly away. Ah... Ah didnae mean it like that, Tink. Ye jist surprised me."

"I felt your disgust," I choke out. One traitorous tear slides down my cheek. "You hated touching me."

"Nae," he says, voice a hushed whisper. "Gods, Tink... ye're the only person Ah *can* touch without losin' me cool. Ah dinnae know if it's magic or if it's

54

just somethin' about ye but..."

He sucks in a deep breath, and I feel a fine tremor run through his arms.

"I don't understand," I start, shaking my head. "When you touched me, I could feel your repulsion."

He nods and then sighs, long and heavy. "Ah need to… explain." Then he grows silent again, seemingly summoning his nerve. "Ah've never had a partner Ah wanted, Tink. Seventeen partners in me life an' Ah never asked a single one o' them to be with me."

"How?" I start, my brows furrowing because I'm not sure I follow.

"Ah've had me only sexual experiences forced on me," he finishes, and there's a vulnerability suddenly in his eyes that makes me want to cry.

"Oh, Quinn," I start, reaching out to touch his cheek. My mortification slips away, to be replaced with a quiet sense of horror. He's been violated? The immortal Quinn? Scourge of pirates? One of the most feared mercenaries of all time?

He shakes his head and grabs my hand mid-air. "Ah dinnae want yer pity," he insists.

I swallow hard as I nod and take my hand back.

He looks to the ground before facing me again. "Whit Ah will ask for… is yer patience. This is all new an' rather novel—this wantin' a woman who wants me back."

"I understand," I offer.

He nods. "The disgust ye felt… 'tis naethin' to do with ye. Ye're lovely an' any man would be lucky to bed ye, but Ah... would rather hold ye like this, if ye dinnae mind."

"I don't mind," I say and bring my hand back to touch his stubbled cheek. This time he doesn't fight me.

A sad smile mangles his lips as he reads my expression. "Do ye think me weak, hardly a man at all?"

"No," I breathe, shaking my head. "Gods, no."

"Then let's find that bower, if ye can stand me. Ah'm done in an' Ah'd like a rest."

I grin at him, the expression sudden, fierce, and unexpected. "There's nothing I'd like better."

SEVEN
QUINN

I wake with a sweet, citrus scent teasing my nose. After weeks of sailing, it's welcome. Neverland waters smell of brine, algae, and rot. The entire principality is dying, one year at a time. Magic ensures we'll never die off entirely, but Gods, we really should. It'd be a mercy if every womb in Neverland closed up and we died off quietly. I pity any child born into this Gods forsaken place.

I curl around the warmth that lays half on top of me. The ground beneath me is soft, the morning air pleasant. I can almost pretend this has all been an awful dream, and I'm about to crack my eyes open and find the silvery foliage of the Enchanted Forest around me. But when I dare to open my eyes, I find the waxy green leaves more at home in an oasis than on the barren rocks of a Neverland Island.

The shape shifts on top of me, making a soft, kitten-like purr of contentment. There's a dainty arm slung over my chest, and soft, downy hair tucked into the crook of my arm. I follow the clean expanse of smooth, olive-toned skin to its owner. Tinker's face is slack with sleep, which makes her appear even younger

than she first seemed. She's apparently sixty-five. She
doesn't look a day over nineteen. Asleep, she looks
closer to eighteen. It's difficult to believe this woman is
one of the Chosen. That she's the last thing standing
between the Seelie and extinction…

Also difficult to believe she propositioned me, and
I turned her down. Like the fool I am. Even now, that
the soft pressure of her body has me hard. I haven't
been hard in ages and can't remember the last time I
found release, even with my own hand. Peter finds
something desirable in every woman. I honestly have
never been able to see the appeal of sex.

Until now.

Her skin is so smooth. Silken, even. The brief
brush against her mound was very thrilling before the
memories of Mistress Chamir rose to choke the stirring
of desire within me. Seeing Tinker now, her face
sparkling with morning dew, I can't think of anything
else.

She stirs again, one slender leg brushing against
my length as she stretches. Her lashes flutter, and then
I'm staring at her from inches away. She's so close, her
warmth so unexpectedly welcome; I can't help myself.
I lean closer, press my lips to hers, rolling her gently
beneath me. Our weight crushes the flowers, sending
their perfume swirling around us.

Her lips form a lush 'o' when I draw away from
her.

"Ah'm sorry," I breathe. "Ah shouldnae have…"

"Don't apologize," she whispers back, leaning in to

punctuate the statement with a brief kiss. She tastes the way she smells: like a twist of orange. Surprisingly sweet. "You can do more if… you want to," she continues with a broad grin. "The offer still stands."

She wiggles enticingly beneath me. Her sage green dress rode up sometime during the night, revealing the soft, perfect swells of her thighs. She's got the proportions of a woman, even though she's barely four feet tall. I'm almost afraid to break her. I have to be three, four times her weight.

Still, I have to admit to some curiosity. My eyes never leaving hers, I get a fistful of her dress and ease it slowly up. My eyes dart down to consider her quim. An uncharacteristic sense of bashfulness seizes me. I never looked at the women I fucked (or more accurately, who fucked me) for more than a few seconds. Often times, not even that. Mistress Chamir would chain my hands and work me to arousal, then mount me like I was some sort of brood mare. I refused to look at her. So it surprises me that I really *do* want to explore Tinker's body and I want to watch myself as I do so.

She's hairless between her legs as well, and I'm curious about the texture. When I smooth my thumb over her mound, I find it silken smooth, just like the rest of her. She shivers, arching up into me. Doing so presses my hardness against her thigh. My arousal makes it hard to think.

"Oh, yes," she breathes. "Lower. Touch me lower, Quinn. Please." She continues to squirm against me. "I haven't been touched in decades..."

59

Decades. The reminder almost makes me laugh. It's easy to forget, with her innocent, delicate appearance, that she's older than I am. She's probably had many lovers before me and knows just what she likes.

"Show me," I whisper. "Show me how ye find yer pleasure, Princess."

Tinker doesn't hesitate. She takes hold of my hand, guides me until I'm cupping her mound. She's so small, I feel like I might break her.

"Thumb here," she demands in a breathy whisper as she places the digit on her erect nub. "And a finger inside."

It's got to be magic or madness because I obey. I sink a finger into her heat and let my thumb come to rest on that small bud. I know from my time with Mistress Chamir, how to manipulate it with my tongue, but I've never used my hand. Mistress Chamir was the queen of her own corner of Avernus, and she made sure I treated her like one. No putting my common, filthy hands on her. Such was why I was so often in chains.

I squeeze my eyes shut and push thoughts of Chamir away. I'm with Tinker, and I won't let visions and memories of that awful woman interrupt me now. No, Tinker deserves far more than that.

Tink lets out a breathy moan when I begin slowly pumping my finger into her. My thumb moves in quick, deft circles. I'm not sure it can feel as good as my tongue would, especially owing to my calloused fingers. *Calloused fingers...* I shouldn't even be touching her because she's a princess and I'm… I'm nothing and no one.

I'm trapped forever in the same skin I wore at nineteen. From the time I could toddle, I'd been on a ship: the cook's assistant at first, then a cabin boy. Eventually, I graduated to a soldier. A life handling rope, scrubbing decks, and mending sails gave me thick calluses. Becoming first a prisoner and then a mercenary did little to soften my hands.

Still, she seems to be enjoying herself. That's strangely... gratifying. Her skin has flushed a light olive green. The sight spurs me on, as does the flutter of her walls around my finger. The moans falling from her lips drive me half mad. I've never wanted a woman. Not like this. Peter's half-convinced I fancy men. Never. Not after Ironcross. I just hadn't found a woman who could drive the thoughts of Mistress Chamir from my head long enough for my body to respond to hers.

Magic.

Tinker is pure magic, and I want a taste of her citrusy, sweet skin. I want to drink her in, feel her tightness around me. The experience, free of horror at last, actually is a heady, orgasmic thing on its own.

Tinker whimpers, arching her body up into mine. Her walls clench tight and her wings flare out around her body, shimmering a brilliant gold as she finds her release. The light sears my eyes, but I catch the look of rapture on her face before I'm forced to close them against the brightness. A warm drop of satisfaction slides into my stomach, warming me from within. I haven't known her long, but there's a haunted shadow lurking behind her eyes. For an instant, I can see her as she's meant to be. Carefree. Just a woman who's found pleasure with a man.

I crack my eyes open, cautious, when the glare no longer turns the inside of my lids red. Tinker is still there, splayed beneath me, curling contentedly like a cat. Her wings are trapped beneath her and I can't resist studying them. I've never seen a Seelie Fae up close before and her wings remind me of dragonfly wings, segmented and shimmering with rainbow patterns in the light. They're dusted with fine green and gold dust.

"Gods ye're beautiful..." I breathe.

She smiles, pleased and a little shy. She knows her own body. More than almost any woman I've seen Peter bed. So many years of living, maybe? And yet, she's been sheltered here on this island with only a cranky giant-croc shifter for company. And apparently that daft bastard refused to touch her because... it's been decades since she felt a man's touch. I almost can't believe it.

It's endearing to realize she's almost as new to this as I am. Being with her is so different from Mistress Chamir, who was all swaying hips, wicked smiles, and coy games. Until she grew tired of the pretense, and then took what she wanted by force. Tinker is none of those things—she's innocence and kindness and blushing awkwardness but somehow together—all those things just feel so right, so candid.

"Your turn," she says, reaching between us to tug

at my belt. I'm still wearing the clothes I arrived in. I even slept with weapons on—this horrid place requires being ready for action at all times.

I tense when she worms her fingers down the front of my trousers. Will she tug at me until I cry out? Mistress Chamir had ways of keeping me hard, even when she caused me great pain.

There's no chance to find out, because, far in the distance, I hear the low hum of whale song. It's the same sort of song that resonated through the waters when we'd breached the island's last defenses. Which can only mean one thing.

We're under attack.

***

ZEGAR

Where the bloody fuck has the princess gotten off to now? If we survive this situation, I will paddle her small, shapely arse from here to the Coves. With a swarm of batmen, hellhounds, and a Priapen female leading the charge, we are in trouble.

The Priapen ascends the hill from the beach to the mainland in a smooth roll of hips, exuding raw sexuality from every pore. There's no denying she's a comely thing. Tall, leggy, with skin that glows like back lit alabaster. She flips a sheet of raven hair over

one shoulder, smile arrogant, so very assured in her
superiority. Her eyes are the perfect teal that oceans
ought to be, but never are in this place. I'm told that
meeting the eyes of a Priapen is like being yanked
under by a riptide. Sudden, frightening, and ultimately
deadly. Most never resurface again.

But giant's blood makes me hard to charm. Even
my shifter side isn't swayed by the magic of a Priapen,
as a human would be. Still, I can appreciate the
woman's aesthetic. Crocodiles are cold and don't attach
to one female for long, but for rare exceptions.

My exception is missing, hidden somewhere on
this damned island. Yes, I'm aware of her private
places she likes to retire to, and I don't bother her when
she needs time alone. I'm beginning to regret not at
least mapping out where she might be, though. Perhaps,
if we live to return to the mainland, I'll buy bells and
sew them onto her slippers, so she'll be easier to track.

The batmen have taken to the air with shrieks that
claw at my ears. Perhaps I've been spoiled by the long
years of solitude. Living without the daily chaos of
Neverland cities, I've grown softer than I like.
Nevertheless, the batmen won't get past me. I'll gush
blood from my ears, nay, every orifice before I let them
lay even a fore-claw on her. Tinker is the closest thing
to a sister I've ever had, and I'll be damned if anything
happens to her.

The smile on the Priapen woman's face grows a
touch less confident when I heft a fallen log and fling it
skyward like I've entered a caber toss match. Three

batmen shriek as the log drives into their middles, sending them backward toward the surf. The lucky ones land in the heaving waves, driven downward by the weight of the log. It won't keep them down for long. Too buoyant.

One unlucky batman clips the edge of the schooner, spine snapping like a brittle twig against the wooden railing. It's flailing, furry legs go slack and all it can do is shriek impotently as it slides from the railing down into the water. The water bubbles for a time, but the thing doesn't resurface.

Pan vaults into the air like he's got springs in his heels, spiraling upward with a crow of satisfaction. As pleased as I am to see him, knowing he's quite a comrade to have at one's back, I do fear he'll take advantage of the princess. Yet, as much as Pan enjoys his mischief, his whoring, and his drink, his first love is and always will be flight. I have no qualms with that. What I do have qualms with, however, is if he tramples the princess' heart. Do that and I will end him, comrade or no.

Pan's leg is still bandaged, though by the way he's moving, I imagine its most probably healed. Good thing, too, because we each need to be in top shape if we're to survive this battle. It's a bloody shame that vampire is as completely useless to us as he is at the moment—buried in the depths of the *Little White Bird*, where he's sound asleep and avoiding the sun, which will kill him.

The leaf-edged blade clears Pan's scabbard with a

ringing sound. Seelie craftsmanship at its finest. Pan
can't miss with that blade. For once, I'm grateful he
won it off me in a bet. He performs another jubilant
curlicue before shooting further into the sky,
disappearing into the vapors. More shrieks filter
through the fumes above us. The sky is no longer toxic
as the dome was destroyed when Pan and his friends
breached it. Now, the sky above us reveals just early
morning cloud cover. If the island's defenses were
functional, these monsters would have met their final
end at the border. I want to curse Pan and Quinn for
placing the princess in so much danger. But I know,
deep down, I can't protect her forever. She's Chosen—
she just doesn't know it yet.

The Priapen woman sidles closer, gliding cat-like
on bare feet. Slender, shapely toes leave impressions in
the sand as she moves, each movement alluring and
graceful. She's undressed up to her thighs. The small
scrap of fabric she wears that covers her femininity can
barely be called an undergarment. A band of leather
keeps her breasts snugged high and tight to her chest,
coyly hiding her nipples. Her chest is flushed pink with
desire and a small, dexterous tongue darts out to touch
her lower lip.

"So strong," she coos as she looks at me, her
glance falling lower. "And your cock is huge! Gods, I
bet you crush mortal women, don't you, shifter?" Her
eyes narrow as she reads me. "Haven't you wondered
what it could be like to fuck someone properly?"

That's the thing about the Priapen. They know

what men and women want, can read their deepest desire like words scrawled plainly on parchment. Even if she doesn't charm me the way she might a mortal man, there's no denying she's right. I've wanted a good romp in the sheets for ages, but given my situation, that experience has never presented itself. And, as I'm Tinker's guardian, I've never thought of her in such a way.

The Priapen woman has a blade in one hand, but it's limp at her side. Her eyes are all for me, one pale hand sliding over the swell of her breasts and down her taut stomach. She toys playfully with the thin cloth that hides her sex from view. Then with a soft, breathy exclamation, she slides two fingers inside the fine fabric and begins to stroke herself. She keeps moving toward me, lust slamming into me in waves. Any other man would be splayed beneath her by now, eyes rolled into his skull as she rides him in a wave of alabaster pale flesh. She'd ride an ordinary man to death within a day or so.

"What did he call you?" she muses, fingers dancing over her bud in an almost mesmerizing motion. Just because I'm not under her spell doesn't mean it isn't damn distracting. "Zegar? Would you like me to call your name while you are buried within me, Zegar?"

"Shut the fuck up, demon," I snarl, stooping to seize a boulder next. It's unwieldy, but it'll do until I can get a great-sword and a crossbow. My homemade spears and bone knives won't end this bitch.

I hurl the boulder with a grunt of effort. The

Priapen moves faster than even my eyes can track, disappearing from view. The boulder impacts where she'd been seconds before, gouging a deep furrow into the wet sand.

When I can pick her out again, she's alighted on the stone, and then she's launched herself gracefully into the air, spiraling toward me. I don't have time to move. The Priapen collides with me in mid-air, long legs lashing around my waist like a pair of steel cords. She rides me to the ground, grinding her front against mine. Despite my best efforts, I'm hard. The impact against the sand barely registers. My body throws up a curious tingling as the giant's formidable constitution fights the pounding lust she's driving into me.

The keen edge of a blade traces my throat and, when I blink the stars from my vision, the Priapen is smirking, her lips inches away from mine. She arches her back like a contented cat, pressing her firm breasts to my chest. Her entire body shudders with anticipation as she rears up over me, reaching between us for my cock.

"Gods," she breathes. "I'm going to enjoy this. I'll take you inch by delicious inch, Zegar. Just the tip at first. Let you feel your first real woman in... ah... fifteen years, has it been? Fuck me hard and well and I may even keep you."

A blast of eye-searing light blazes through the air above me, setting stars dancing across my vision again. The weight of the Priapen disappears, lifted from me like a leaf in a strong gale. By the time I'm able to blink things into focus again, the air above me is swirling white vapor, dancing in and out of the pines. If I strain, I think I can make out the blurred vision of Pan still weaving in and out of the clouds, fighting his last opponent. Things are eerily still and quiet, as though even the forest sucked in its breath.

"I don't think so, bitch," Tinker snarls into the silence.

I crane my neck, searching desperately for my missing charge and find her eight feet up, wings a golden-green blur of motion, her sage dress rumpled from sleep, hair loose and tousled. She seems to glow from within, a furious inner light that I've only seen once before, when she saved my life. She never exerts herself magically unless she has no other choice. She's never admitted the reason aloud, but I can guess.

Guilt.

Gnawing, clawing guilt for a very human (to pardon the grossly speciest term) mistake.

Now, she looks magnificent. Every inch a faerie queen.

Then the glow begins to dim, her fire doused by doubt and the sudden realization that she's utilizing her magic. She sags and would have slumped to the ground without Quinn there to catch her. He looks rumpled, too. A thought rears as ugly and toxic as a viper in the back of my head.

Has he deflowered her?

No, surely not. I'd believe Pan could coax his way under her skirts in a matter of hours, but not Quinn.

Silent, stoic Quinn who barely touches himself, let alone anyone else. After the rat-faced bastard he'd called 'brother' sold him into slavery, sexual and otherwise, I doubt he feels like touching a woman again in his lifetime.

So why does he look flushed and a little shamefaced?

No time to ruminate over it now. We have to escape this Gods forsaken rock before Agatha sends more troops. This was a minor incursion, a taster of what Agatha can bring to bear. She'd sent no more soldiers than she was willing to lose to the vapors, but if they spied Peter dueling the batmen above the vapor line, we're about to be swamped in the bloody things.

Finding my feet is difficult after the direct assault by the Priapen. She almost managed to crack my defenses. Whether I like it or not, I need to bed a woman when we reach Fantasia. If I weren't so hard-up, the Priapen would have had little to no effect on me at all.

My arousal wedges between my breeches and my thigh, so hard it hurts to move. Tough shit. We have to move and move fast.

"To the *Little White Bird.*" My voice comes out surprisingly level, though I feel like I've been swimming for miles. I'm inexplicably exhausted, and everything below my waist aches. "We have to leave now, Princess."

But Tinker isn't looking at me. I'm not entirely sure she's listening. She has one trembling hand pressed to her mouth, shining tears brimming over and spilling down her cheeks. I follow her gaze and understand precisely what has upset her.

The tree the Priapen woman impacted has a hole through the center of the trunk and leans into its neighbor like a whispering lush. The Priapen is worse off. At first, the mind doesn't register that kind of carnage, tries to preserve your sanity by making an abstract pattern of it. Anything so you don't see, so you don't understand. Then the picture resolves itself and the horrible truth is there, staring back at you.

The Priapen's body has been turned inside out, naked bleeding flesh curled around hair, teeth, and bone, like an enormous, festering teratoma. This doesn't look like Seelie magic. Seelie magic does not easily kill, and Tinker has already taken life once. She mutters about it in her sleep, the doubt that she's truly Seelie. Another time, I'll scrub those tears away and tell her killing is a part of every court, light and dark. But there's no time for soft words or comforting embraces now. The whale song continues to thrum through the water. There are more coming.

"Pan!" I call up to him. "Get the princess to the ship!"

"On it!" he responds.

He descends from the clouds, graceful as a lark, and snatches Tinker from midair like an avaricious gull, spiriting her into the night sky.

I spare one last glance at the Priapen woman and allow myself a shudder.

Then I'm off, zipping through the trees and toward Tinker's ship, ignoring the ache in my balls and the doubt in my own heart.

EIGHT
PETER

Tinker's feet impact the deck of the *Little White Bird* with soft thumps before folding immediately under her. She collapses to the ground, shoulders shaking with sobs. I suppose I can understand why she's distraught. The Priapen demoness was a sight to see at the very end. Nothing she didn't deserve, of course, but perhaps the sight was more than a lady's gentle constitution can take. After all, the Seelie were often pacifists. Violence and death don't come naturally to the light Fae.

"Down below," I order. "If you can't fight, at least get out of the kill zone."

It's the tone more than the words that draw her head up in surprise. Leader I may be, but Quinn's more diplomatic than I am any day ending in Y. Usually, my mouth opens with the best of intentions yet codswallop, mockery, and curses tumble out instead. Sad to say I *am usually* being diplomatic. Yet, I can't bring myself to mock a girl so fragile-looking.

Her fragility is an illusion, of course. She's probably got more strength in her pinkie than a grown man, and she's brimming up to her pointy ears in magic. With the death of the Priapen, Tinker's already proved she's damned powerful. The trick is getting her to see that strength in herself.

"Don't be an ass," she snaps at me, her biting words surprising as I have yet to see her angry. She swipes a hand under her nose, holding back another sniffle as her jaw goes tight, and she stands up as tall as she's able. "This is *my* ship. It needs *my* magic to fly and, therefore, I'll call the orders."

Good girl. "Then up to the helm with you and let's set off. I'd rather not be here when the rest of Agatha's troops arrive. What say you?"

"Aye, aye," she says, a wavering smile alighting on her lovely lips. She gives me the barest of salutes and then her wings blur into motion again, lifting her from the deck. She glides to the helm, trailing green and gold sparks as she goes. Where the sparks hit the deck, carved sigils begin to glow. I can tell this ship fairly thrums with power. The craftsmanship is superb. Not only the intricate spell work, but the construction itself. I'd even wager it's more of a beaut than Hook's *Jolly Roger*, which I heard was finally sunk near Delorood. Serves him right. He's a fucking bastard and always will be. Men who sell their own blood to monsters don't change and they don't deserve to.

The ship lifts from the sand, groaning like a tired old man as its bones stretch for the first time in an age. Payne has been of little use to us and continues to be of little use as he snoozes through all the commotion, deep within the belly of the *Little White Bird*. Bloody useless undead.

The ship hovers a few feet from the ground, brushing the lowest branches of the nearest pines, when Zegar and Quinn burst into the clearing. They're being tailed by more batmen, and only maintain a small lead because the batmen can't extend their wings fully in the dense maze of pine trunks. Their jaws snap closed inches behind Quinn's back, flecks of spittle spraying the nape of his neck. His cry is equal parts fear and disgust.

Zegar spins when they clear the trees, seizes Quinn by his slim shoulders, and hurls him like a javelin. Quinn lets out a comical sound as he arcs toward the deck of the *Little White Bird*. I've been fiddling with the ropes, trying to get the sails down, but I'm little better on a ship than Quinn. I'm already plunging to his rescue when he manages to roll in midair and come to a shuddering stop just before he'd have scraped himself raw on the deck. He throws his hands out, wobbling, trying desperately to find balance. Quinn was never much good at flying, either.

Tink must have given him some of her pixie dust, because he's never touched a spark of Saxe's magic.

Quinn glances up uncertainly at the helm, eyeing Tink's position at the wheel. There's something very like tenderness in his eyes, there for only a split second, but very raw and real.

Moon's bloody left teat! Can this mean what I think it means? Has Quinn finally fucked a woman at last? And a faerie princess, no less! I'm torn between the desire to clap him on the back or box his ears. It's not often I'm bested, and any man with eyes would have seen I wanted her for myself.

Bugger.

Zegar vaults the ship's railing by a narrow margin and sprawls on deck in a graceless heap. I can't help but smirk at him. It's the fucking third leg he's packing in his trousers that's slowed his gait and made it difficult for him to move at all. I'm not a lover of men, but even I have a difficult time keeping my eyes from it. It's one of those sights you can't help but stare at. It's *that* big.

"Are you smuggling a bear cub in your pants, Zegar?" I chirp, flashing him a would-be innocent smile.

Zegar's already rough-hewn face creases down into a ferocious scowl, and I see a hint of the crocodile in his eyes. The low rumble of his beast's warning call builds in his chest, a rattling bass sound that ends on a hiss. The sound raises hairs at the back of my neck. My body tends to be saner than I am, on any given day.

"Don't fuck with me, Pan," he says, and his voice sounds like it's been dragged over a mile of gravel. He's changing, scales pebbling on his skin, pushing out, extruding until they're rough and three dimensional. His body morphs slowly with horrific snapping and slurping sounds, until an enormous crocodile stands in his place.

I grin down at the crocodile, unable to help myself. "Fuck with you, Zegar? Why, I wouldn't even know where to begin, old chap! Do crocodiles even have bollocks?"

Zegar lunges and snaps at empty air. He'd have caught my ankle if I hadn't taken to the sky, a safe twelve feet up. I've seen him leap to catch food before. Watching him snatch Hook's hand will forever be a treasured memory. Given Zegar's mood now, he'd probably turn me into peg-leg, to compliment my rival's 'hook'.

Zegar has a strong sense of irony.

I understand his reasoning, though. That Priapen almost had him dead to rights, despite a giant's near immunity to sexual charm. It's clear as day he needs a fuck (don't we all?)—otherwise the Priapen wouldn't have nearly taken control of him. At least in his current form, any other Priapens will have to actively search for his bait and tackle. All puns intended.

Priapen tastes are strange. I can't say if they'd want a go with a croc or not. Probably difficult to get around the teeth, I'd wager.

"Alright, alright!" I say with a laugh. "Settle yourself at the helm, you scaly bastard. I'll be up in the crow's nest. Quinn, can you run out the long nines?"

Quinn jerks at the mention of his name, boots settling onto the deck at last. He blinks rapidly, swallows hard and then gives one jerky nod.

"O' course. Like the job we finished in Ironcross?"

"Right you are, Quinn, my boy. Let's show Agatha we still have steel balls, eh?"

Quinn rolls his eyes, breathing out a sigh of

deepest exasperation. Yes, cannonballs are made of iron. But 'balls of iron' doesn't carry the same dramatic weight. If I were born in any place but Neverland, I'd have been a star—I'm quite convinced. Quinn says I've got less talent than I seem to believe of myself, but everyone's a critic.

We ascend quickly with Tink at the wheel, steering us expertly through the cloud bank and into the sooty air over Marwolaeth Island.

The air had been comparatively sweet low on the island, insulated as it was from the choking miasma that is the rest of Neverland. It's almost a shame we had to breach the vapors. It was nice to see one island not ravaged by war. Whether we live to escape this blasted principality or are devoured by batmen, one thing is certain: Marwolaeth Island will be deforested, strip mined, and squabbled over for years to come. Peace won't come to Neverland until it's scoured with fire or the land is swallowed by the sea.

There's a soft bed of blankets in the bowl-like crow's nest and a bound book peeks out from under a straw-stuffed pillowcase. I tug it loose, examine it in the briefest of moments before we truly get underway. It's a leather-bound journal. The book opens easily (no locks to keep the contents closed), and I can tell she reads the tale inside often.

Peter and His Lost Boys it reads. *Transcribed from the oral accounts of a grumpy crocodile.*

I choke on a laugh, and fight not to puff out my chest like an arrogant cock. It isn't the time to get a

78

swelled head. Still, the thought that she's heard as much about us as we have about her... it's gratifying. Intensely so. Not a wonder she took Quinn to her bed. He must be her hero.

Discordant cries carry on the wind to us, and I crane my neck up in time to spy a formation of the wretched batmen swooping down from the sooty cloud cover. They plummet toward the deck, aiming for our small captain. I drop the book and get a firmer grip on my sword, swinging it into guard position.

The long nine's report is deafening and rocks the ship. The cannons aren't secured well. Not Tink's fault, of course. She had no idea we were coming for her, and we'd planned a smoother departure than this. Damn the vampire for being nocturnal. We could really use another set of hands on the guns. Quinn's only got two hands. He can't man both sides.

The cannonball slams through their line, breaking the formation so they'll be easier to pick off. The bottom half of several batmen just disappear in a spray of blood and viscera. Ropey gray intestines stream from one of the nearest, as it drops to the deck, impacting with a wet thump. It trails blood and shit like foul mayday ribbons around the mast. Its batlike head bursts open upon impact, spattering Quinn's back with gray matter, even from a distance. His back stiffens as a glob of the stuff slides down the collar of his frock coat.

Something goes spinning out of the hands of the batman, shattering to pieces when it strikes the cabin door. Black smoke plumes out, whipped away almost at once by the increasing speed of the *Little White Bird.*

The ship has picked up speed, and I'm forced to doff my hat, shoving it between the breastplate and my undershirt for safekeeping. We're ascending, up and up, so that the moon glows just above me like a vast silver medallion. If I reach up, I half fancy I could capture it. The air up this high ought to be cold, but it's not. All of Neverland is warm, like a feverish hand with a stranglehold on the entire place—it chokes the life from us incrementally year after year. Sweat already pops from my brow and gathers in slick lines beneath the armor.

But... no. This is *too* hot, even for Neverland. It reminds me of the blistering heat of the Anoka Desert or the hot, sulfurous breath of a...

Hellhound.

A glance down confirms my worst fears. The smoke disappeared, but the fire is eating into the deck, stubborn cinders determined to take root and set the whole ship ablaze. The batmen aren't aiming to swarm us. They just need to douse us in hellfire.

Fucking son of a whore. Last we were here, the witch bitch, Agatha, only had batmen at her disposal. But now she's created hellhounds... or borrowed them. Hmm, she must have bargained with Morningstar's generals for the hellhounds in return for Hook's return. She's infatuated with the fucking prick. Gods only know why. If I could guarantee safe passage for the princess, I'd hand Hook to the sorceress spit-roasted and slathered with honey.

Zegar leaps, dragging a batman from midair, gnashing his middle to pulp with dagger-like teeth. It squeals, still living, and tries to stab the crocodile with its own bottle of liquid fire. The blows glance easily off Zegar's scales. Quinn is still gunning down more formations. Payne will be no help, asleep as the bastard is. It's up to me to put the damned fire out.

It takes a distressingly long time to free a sail and longer to trail it in the sea, bringing it up sodden and stained gray. Smoke immediately curls up when the wad of wet fabric settles over the conflagration. One, solitary spark jumps from the air to my skin, working its way into one of the small cuts I sustained during the first incursion.

The second it makes contact with my skin, my blood catches fire, roiling into a fine boil. Blackness slides like viscous blood over my eyes, slides like water down my throat and up my nose, choking off my air.

I collapse to the deck.

There's a hideous sound echoing back to me, a tortured scream.

And I realize, with horror, it's mine.

NINE
TINKER

Peter's veins pulse a solid black and show vividly against the ivory of his skin. I trace the pad of my thumb over the straining line of his brachial artery. The map of veins stands out like striations in marble. Sweat pools in the bends of his elbows, his knees, and beneath his arms. He's too hot to the touch. Far, far too warm to still cling to life. He's being boiled to death from the inside out.

And none of us have any idea how to save him. We can only watch, impotent, as he writhes in obvious pain and fear. We've already employed the mediocre stores I had on board. An island colloquially known as 'Death Isle' among the locals isn't flush with healing herbs and salves. Ultimately, it's only Zegar's foul, fermented pine drinks that have kept Peter from screaming himself hoarse. Keeping him too piss drunk to scream is a poor option, but it's the only one we have.

We've kept the ship moving in shifts, Zegar, Quinn, and I rotating who's steering the ship toward the Neverland falls. We've been forced to move slower, using the sooty clouds as camouflage. We can't afford another incident with the batmen. Not until we know for certain what's been done to Peter.

Payne is on deck now that what wavering sunlight Neverland boasts has disappeared behind the western horizon. The moon gleams through the porthole in the captain's quarters, illuminating Peter's flushed face. He looks physically younger when his face is slack. Far too young to be fifty-nine.

"There has to be somethin' we can do," Quinn says, pacing the room. He's been on his feet for over an hour, pacing in furious circles, as though he can somehow stomp the answers out of the deck. "If he continues to roon this hot, he'll die. Mayhap we ought to doonk him in the water."

Zegar has hunkered down in the corner, keeping his long, well-muscled legs curled tight to his body, doing his best to hide his cock from view. He burst out of his clothing during the battle and hasn't found anything aboard the *Little White Bird* that will double as proper clothing. Quinn offered him the clumsily stitched tablecloth I'd made a year ago, suggesting he use it as a kilt. Zegar, in response, casually backhanded Quinn's bicep hard enough to bruise. Apparently, Zegar prefers to stroll around nude, rather than wear the stitched together remains of Neverland flags I'd fished from the sea and I guess I can't blame him for it.

"What do you suggest?" Zegar asks, curling a little closer to the wall. His voice still holds a deep rasp, as if he hasn't come all the way back from his crocodile form. The way his eyes track Quinn's progress across the room is nothing short of reptilian. At any moment, I expect him to lunge for Quinn's ankles.

"Maybe I should attempt to suck the venom from him?" Payne asks.

Zegar shakes his head. "That will just bring the venom into you and the last thing we need is a vampire hellhound on our hands."

"Hmm," Payne says as his jaw goes tight.

"Is there no cure for this… infection?" I ask, as I look up at Zegar.

He shrugs. "The physician of Sweetland created the disease with Agatha's blood, thus I would assume he's the only one who can create the antidote."

"Then Peter is destined to become a hellhound?" I ask, my voice breaking.

"There has to be a way to fight this," Payne says.

"Aye, there is. Magic," Quinn answers, rounding on me. His eyes show white around the edges, panicked like a horse about to bolt. Like Peter, he looks younger when his guard is down.

I understand what he's asking, and I immediately shake my head. "My magic is too dangerous, Quinn. It's unpredictable and it could end up killing Peter just as easily as it might cure him."

Quinn doesn't look convinced. "Please, Tink. We're all out o' options." He looks over at his friend. "He's dying anyway, so if yer magic kills him, 'twill hurry the process that's already comin' for him." He looks back at me. "But, there's still the chance ye could cure him."

I shake my head again, visions of the last time I

used magic coming back to haunt me. "You saw what I did to the Priapen," I say.

He nods and swallows hard. "Ah did, but ye were defendin' Zegar. Ye were usin' defensive magic then, Tink, nae curin' magic."

"And who's to say they aren't one and the same?"

He shakes his head and then hesitates a moment before he faces me squarely. "You're one o' the Chosen Ten, Tink. Yer powers must be extraordinary… they *are* extraordinary."

"Chosen Ten?" I repeat, shaking my head. "What are you talking about?"

"He's right," Zegar pipes up from where he's sitting across the way. "You are Chosen, Tinker."

I look at him and narrow his eyes. "I thought the Chosen were always just fairy tales?"

"They arenae jist fairy tales," Quinn points out.

I keep my eyes on Zegar. "You told me countless stories about the Chosen, but you never once told me they were real."

"They are real," he insists.

"Then why did you never tell me that? And why did you never tell me I was one of them, if you knew it all this time?" Anger begins to lace my tone.

He breathes in deeply. "I don't have an answer for you… other than I was nervous that if you knew what you were… you might take liberties you shouldn't. And I was afraid of Agatha finding you—I was worried she would discover what you were. So I thought… I thought if I kept it hidden from you, perhaps no one might ever discover… the truth."

"You decided to hide me from the world," I finish for him.

He nods. "I was planning on telling you, eventually."

"Magic," Peter whispers as his fingers slide free of mine, and it isn't until my back hits the far wall of the cabin that I realize I streaked away from him as fast as my wings would allow. The top of my head collides painfully with the ceiling.

"No!"

The answer is immediate and unthinking. No. I absolutely can't do magic—I don't care what I am or what I'm not. I ought to carve my wings from my back and forget I have this wretched 'gift'. And if it's true that I am one of the Chosen, I've been chosen for the wrong reasons. My magic isn't pure and it isn't good. It's dark and it's laced with murder. It's death magic.

Even the controlled magic I've used on the ship was a risky venture, something I only managed because the charms were small and done over the course of years. A healing like this would take concerted will. I don't trust myself to direct magic at an enemy, let alone an ally. The image of the Priapen's insides will haunt me until my dying day. The adipose tissue shedding blood, intestines tied into knots, the teeth and mandible sticking out from the lumpy mass in gleaming white in the tortured red ball of flesh...

"No," I repeat, more quietly this time. "No, I can't." I can't do that to Peter. I would never forgive myself and I could never live with the consequences.

Quinn crosses the deck quickly, tugging insistently on my slippered foot when I don't immediately float to the ground to face him. His pleading eyes flick from my face to Peter's.

"Please, Tink… ye are his only hope. Ah cannae do this. Zegar sure as feck can't do it. An' Payne is useless."

"Excuse me," Payne mutters, but no one pays him any mind.

"If somethin' isnae done soon, Peter will die."

"If I try to heal him, he'll only die sooner. I can't perform Seelie healing magic, Quinn. I can't… I'm not what… I'm not what any of you think I am."

The broken confession wrenches its way from my throat. It scrapes my throat raw, like it dug glass fingers into my flesh on the way out.

"Whit we think ye are?" Quinn asks, frowning. "Whit do ye mean?"

And this is the point where the truth has to come out, because he has to understand. They all have to understand. I'd rather admit to my horrid nature than do to Peter what I did to the Priapen. "Because I've killed anyone I ever used it on!"

"The Priapen demon was—" Zegar starts.

"I killed my Aunt Saxe!"

It feels like I've been curled around those words for years. Though the memory makes me ill, there's an odd sense of euphoria that accompanies telling the truth at last. I glance to Zegar first, and his stern expression barely wavers. He's never asked and I've never confessed. Still, he knew. He's probably heard my agonized confessions while I've been asleep during all those cold nights when we were forced to huddle close to one another on a cot in the bowels of the ship. I've always been talkative—even in my sleep.

The tension between my shoulder blades lessens by a degree. Zegar knows, but he won't condemn me. He's always been too good to me. And I don't deserve his goodness—not when I'm as dark as the Priapen. Truly, I'm no better.

It's difficult to shift my eyes back to Quinn, but I do. I force myself to gaze into those deep, penetrating eyes. He stares back, frowning at me, but the look on his face is understanding, not accusatory.

I swipe a hand beneath my nose, dirtying the sleeve of my frock. I sink slowly to the cabin floor, my energy washed away like suds after rain.

"But Saxe is," Payne starts, but Quinn looks over at him and shakes his head before returning his gaze to me.

"How?" he asks.

I clutch myself tight, squeezing my eyes shut against the memory. Isn't it bad enough I relive it in my nightmares, night after night? Must I recount it during my waking hours as well? Maybe this is my punishment. Confess my sin before the last person I want to disappoint. The fates do have wicked senses of humor.

I reach into the interior pockets of my dress for the

sending stone. I always keep it close, as a reminder not to be complacent. It leaves sooty imprints on my fingers when I draw it out. It once resembled a smooth blue river stone, buffed, and shined until I could spy my reflection on its surface. Now it's pitted, rough, and as black as pitch. It would have burned along with Aunt Saxe.

"Do you know what this is?" I ask, holding it up for him to see.

Quinn squints at it. "Coal?"

"It used to be a sending stone. They're rare and incredibly hard to make. It was a gift from Aunt Saxe, so I could keep in contact with her. She'd check in monthly, at first. Then every six months. And finally, it reached a point where I was lucky to get an annual talk with her." My voice falters and I have to find the strength within myself to continue. Quinn, meanwhile, has gone very still and quiet, his expression closed and guarded. There's a horrible certainty in his eyes, like he knows what's coming next. He doesn't interrupt, letting me tell the tale in full. I'm grateful, though I'm not certain how to continue. I force my mouth open and then the words just pour like bilge from a ship's hull, messy and full of foul secrets.

"Aunt Saxe had told me the principalities were planning to seal the Great Evil with the lives of human witches. And she told me she wouldn't be able to visit me or talk to me for a while. And… I was so selfish, Quinn. I railed at her, told her she'd never really loved me at all. I accused her of holding me captive on this awful island to usurp my throne. That she'd made me a political prisoner and turned Marwolaeth Island into my prison. The more she tried to reason with me, the angrier I became until..."

My fingers flex around the charred rock. Tears squeeze painfully from the corners of my eyes and roll down my cheeks. "I flung a curse at her—I was just so angry, I couldn't stop myself. I couldn't... control myself. I just meant to show her my anger. I never meant to... I never meant to kill her. I just wanted her to feel the pain I was in. And I... I burned her with faerie fire, Quinn!" I finish as I look up at him, the tears falling freely now. Still, he says nothing.

"Faerie fire?" Payne repeats.

I nod, but I won't look at him. "It's a forbidden Unseelie spell. It causes the recipient's own magic to combust. I didn't even know the spell, so I don't understand how it came out of my mouth. To this day, I don't understand. I didn't mean for it to happen and I couldn't stop it once it had and then..."

First one sob, then another wrench themselves from my chest. I curl into the ship wall, burying my face in my hands. The memory is choking. The sending stones communicate everything. Touch, taste, sight, smell, and feel. I felt the heat radiate off Aunt Saxe as she burned. I can still taste the flavor of her pain as it leaked off her. Though it didn't curl a single hair on her head, she burned. She burned and burned until there was almost nothing left of her. Then, and only then, did the stone catch fire. True fire that left a circular scar in my right palm for many, many years.

"Tink..." Quinn's voice is gentle.

He settles into the stretch of wall next to me and lifts me without effort onto his lap. I feel like a child being comforted after a nightmare. His broad, calloused hands sink into my hair, easing them through the mussed locks. He's careful not to tug as he brushes my hair with his fingers. It's soothing. Something my mother might have done.

"'Tis nae yer fault," he whispers.

"Of course it's my fault! I cast the spell!"

"Without knowin' yer full power," he argues, shaking his head. "Without knowin' how Morningstar tainted it."

"Morningstar?" I repeat, confused. "What does he have to do with this?"

Quinn nods. "If we'd had more time, Peter an' Ah would've explained it to you. Princess Carmine o' Ascor discovered the origins of the Chosen, Tink."

"I don't understand," I say as I clear my eyes and look up at him.

"When Morningstar was wounded in battle, the winds stole his blood an' brought it to the worthy, marking them as his equals. There are five known Chosen thus far. All o' 'em struggle with their powers, Tink. At least a portion o' yer magic is rooted in Morningstar. 'Tis bound to be unpredictable, cruel, an' even..."

"Evil, just like Morningstar, himself?"

Quinn shakes his head as I lean into his arms,

91

resting my head on his well-muscled chest as the meaning sinks in. I can't change what I've done. I can't take back Aunt Saxe's death. But when my powers began to emerge, I'd had doubts as to who and what I truly was. Had I been an Unseelie Fae, swapped at birth? Surely no Seelie Fae could have appetites so dark or powers so volatile. And now everything starts to make more sense—I have Morningstar's power in me. No wonder I killed Aunt Saxe in a fit of desperation and anger. I truly am rotten to my core. Dizziness threatens to drag me under.

"You're nae evil, Tink. None o' us can help the circumstances oonder which we came to be. Ye were infected with evil, but that doesnae *make* ye evil. You're destined for great things an' jist as there is Morningstar's power inside ye, there's goodness an' white magic within ye too." He takes a breath. "Ah know ye can heal Peter."

I have to scrub my eyes hard to see him through the haze of tears. I hate collapsing like this. I don't feel I've earned this grief. Aunt Saxe died at *my* hands. So why am I the one who weeps?

"What if I can't heal him?"

Quinn shrugs. "If we could talk to him, he'd say he'd prefer to die tryin' than fade away quietly." I nod because Quinn's right—that's exactly what Peter would say.

Quinn faces me again. "Whit do ye say?"

What can I say? He's absolutely right. The great Peter Pan did not submit to pirates, to mercenaries, to

92

sirens, or even to almost certain death. He'd rather I slash his throat now than let him die sniveling.

"Alright," I say, even as I can't believe my own words. "I will try."

TEN
PETER

It feels like I'm running through the eight concentric spirals of Avernus, trying to get away from the damned hellhound.

I can't see it lurking in the darkness, but I can hear its huffing breath. The only contrast to the never-ending dark is the occasional leap of sparks when the mutt's nails send up sparks on the rocky ground. I suck in lungfuls of sulfurous air, choke, and cough it back out again. Either I'm dreaming or I'm dead and in eternal torment because every part of me burns. Constant liquid fire shoots through my veins, and there's not even the mercy of unconsciousness to ease the pain.

All I can do is run. Because if the hellhound catches me, I won't survive. Even if I do manage to survive, it won't be in any form I'm familiar with—the evil of the beast will change me—morph me into some equally repulsive creature like all those poor sots Agatha and Septimus have already turned. I'd rather die.

Its thoughts whisper through my head, scraping the inside of my head like iron nails.

Let me wear your skin, boy.

"Not fucking happening," I mutter.

The problem is, I can't see it to outmaneuver it. And I can't even say for sure where *here* even is. My own fevered mind or some other plane? The fuck if I know. It ultimately doesn't matter. All that does matter is preserving my skin, in a very literal fashion. I quite like my skin. No one else will wear it half as well as I do.

My foot meets empty air on the next loping step and I topple over the edge of an unseen cliff. The mutt chuffs a laugh behind me. Mocking me, the canine bastard. I get the feeling he can see in this place, even though I can't.

The wind that buffets me from below is warm, and I hear a faint crackling sound, like logs shifting in the hottest bits of the fireplace.

Great. Off the cliff face and into the fire. What have I done to deserve this?

Want me to list the reasons? That snide, sneering voice that always reminds me of my father asks. Of course I don't want to know the reasons, but he lists them anyway. He always did like detailing my faults when drunk. I never shed one tear when he choked to death on his own vomit in the gutter one night.

You're a strutting peacock who can't keep his dick in his pants. You led your band of boys into a trap and got them all cursed. You didn't end Hook when you had the chance. You're an arrogant, selfish, son of a bitch who wants to steal Quinn's woman...

"Alright, that's enough of you," I mutter to no one

95

in particular.

This place may very well be Avernus. I can't call on flight. I can't even tell if there's a sky above me, or if it's just a dense cloud of vapor. The best I can do is windmill my arms pathetically and shift myself just enough that I don't land in the lapping lake of fire beneath.

Instead, I impact sand. Face first.

Pain spiderwebs through my face, feeling like I've shattered every fine bone. When I manage to flop onto my back and lift my hands to inspect the damage, my nose has the consistency of a mashed tomato.

"My face," I lament, only half-joking. I'm not certain why, but in times of woe, irony seems to be my bedfellow. "My beautiful face..."

"You were only mildly pretty, Pan," a soft, female voice lilts from somewhere above me.

It's hard to focus, but a soft, gold-green light floats above me, wavering and unreal like the glow of a distant Will-o'-the-Wisp. It's entrancing, and I try to raise a hand to capture it. Even the mutt following me pauses, watching the light bob and weave impatiently in the air above.

"Touch me, Peter," the voice says.

"Who are you?" I call back. "Where are you?"

She doesn't respond, instead continues in that soft, lilting voice. "We need to touch, mind to mind, if this is going to work."

"If *what* is going to work?"

I swear her voice sounds familiar, though I can't

place why.

"Touch me, Peter."

"I'm trying," I mumble. Blood dribbles from between my teeth. I probably bit my lip to pieces on impact with the sand. Maybe slamming into the fiery lake would have been less painful in the end.

"Where are you?" I call out, seeing the light bobbing here, then there.

"You're feet away from me, Peter."

"There are two of you then," I grouse. "You keep moving."

A soft sigh breezes over me. Citrusy, sweet and enticing, it reminds me of the air around Delorood. I haven't been there in ages. The closest I've come was the meeting with Goldy in Denfur and Denfur is a ways away from the ocean.

"Just... keep your hand steady, Peter. I'll try to make first contact."

I struggle to follow her instructions, partly mesmerized by the Fae dust sprinkling down toward me, but mostly horrified that the hellhound might be coming near again. I struggle to see it in the haze that surrounds me. But, there's nothing.

"Peter! Focus!" the voice commands and I listen, steadying myself the best I can, considering how my body is falling apart, oozing away. I can only imagine I'm a goner.

You should be so lucky, the hellhound growls. *We've still got a lot of games to play, you and I. You'll be melting away for an eternity.*

"I've got you, Peter," the woman says. "Hang on. Stay with me. Stay with my voice and don't let go of my hand. No matter what. Don't let go of my hand."

Her hand is tiny in mine, but it somehow brings me comfort all the same, like a cooling elixir that flows through my veins and extinguishes the agonizing fire inside me. The fire is still there, of course, burning through my core, slowly creeping outward to consume me whole. The haze around me begins to shatter, to break apart. I can see cracks as the hellhound bays relentlessly, sounding alarmingly close at heel.

Another voice sounds, seemingly even further away. And I recognize it. I know that voice—that deep, Scottish accent. But, who...

Quinn. Quinn is here! Is he running from the hellhound, as well? I try to call out to him, but I can no longer find my voice.

"Tink, we're fallin'. The boat is crackin' apart. Ye have to let go," Quinn is saying. He sounds anxious.

"No. I have him! I have him, Quinn. I just need more time!"

"Ye have to let go. We're capsizing!"

"Is Quinn here too?" I ask, realizing it's Tink holding my hand and she's somehow in my mind. The words come out garbled to my ears, but she seems to understand.

"No," she replies. "It's just you and me here, Peter. You just keep holding my hand—don't think about anything else but that."

"Tink!" Quinn calls, more urgent this time.

A loud noise shatters the gray fog around us, splitting it open as the hellhound bellows angrily, his screeches filling the void even as it closes behind me. I'm catapulted out of the bowels of Avernus and back into the confines of the ship, my body lying on a small cot and I face the wooden beams of the ceiling above. The heat begins to subside.

"Am I hideous? Am I melted?" I ask.

"Nae, Peter. Ye're fine, ye vain twat," Quinn groans as he looks about the boat, and I realize it's just as whole as it was before.

"You said it was capsizing?" I ask.

He shrugs. "An' so it was, yet once Tink rescued ye, it seems she rescued the ship."

"It was all just in our heads," Tink announces as she looks from me to Quinn, then back again. "None of it was real—just artifice, meant to confuse us."

I look at Quinn, but realize he's not looking back at me. Instead, he's focused on Tink as she floats above us, her gold-green dust sprinkling all about as she steadies the badly shaking ship. Like a blur, she flies out of the room as the boat shifts to one side, sending me shooting onto the floor below. A moment passes and the ship steadies, Zegar stumbling into the room with an angry scowl.

"Where is Tinker?" he barks at us.

I struggle to my feet and almost fall down again, but Quinn catches me.

"Whoa, take it easy, Peter." Then he turns to face Zegar. "Ah'll go find Tink."

"I'll find *Tink*. You two have done enough," Zegar growls, eying Quinn with particular ire.

It would seem I'm not the only one who knows about what went on between Quinn and the lovely Fae guiding our ship. I've no intention of mentioning it, though I'm full of questions. I had been certain I would be the one to crawl between her legs first. Good on Quinn for beating me to the punch, but I can't help but feel a tiny bit green.

As Quinn disappears from the room, heavy on Zegar's heels despite Zegar's obvious disdain, I lay back down on the cot, my head still swimming. I might make light of it to my shipmates, but I'd been in more agony than anything I'd ever experienced in my exceptionally long life. Even the injuries I'd sustained during the Forever War hadn't felt as bad as the sensation of burning alive from the inside out. No, nothing compares to being consumed by a hellhound. I collapse onto the bed and close my eyes, grateful to drop into the depths of slumber.

***

When I awake, Tinker is beside me, watching me as I blink the sleep away from my eyes. We are below deck, in the captain's quarters, as far as I can tell.

"Welcome back again," she says with a soft smile.

"Thanks. I mean, thanks to you. The fire would have taken me if you hadn't come for me. I don't know what happened."

"It was caused by the batmen. I think they meant to turn you into a hellhound."

I ponder this for a moment, nodding. "How long have I been out?"

"All night," she answers.

"Then is it day?"

"It's morning," she answers as she gives me a smile. "There's been a plague in Sweetland. They're calling it 'The Razing'. It's caused by Agatha and Septimus—they've been spreading this disease to the townspeople and it turns them into batmen and hellhounds. At least, that's the story Zegar's been feeding me."

"It's true," I answer.

"I didn't know Agatha and Septimus had fire magic at their disposal," she continues, as she holds a wet compress to my forehead, gingerly patting it.

"They don't."

"Then who—" she starts, but I interrupt her.

"The Lycaon."

"But, he's been dead," she says, but I interrupt again with a shake of my head.

"He's not dead. I think he's found a new body and is building an army of hellhounds with the help of Agatha and your uncle."

"And the physician of Sweetland who created this disease in the first place."

"Right," I answer as I wiggle my toes and fingers and I'm pleased to find they both respond. Apparently, I've survived the toss with the hellhound and I have

101

Tink to thank.

"Then they have to be stopped," Tink says. "And so does this plague—if we could somehow reverse this disease, we would basically take out Agatha and Septimus' army."

"Yes," I say as I stare at her pointedly. "But, as to how we do that is anyone's guess."

"We would have to go to Sweetland—find that physician and demand he reverse it—demand he create a cure that can save the people and return them to their normal state." Then she worries her lower lip and shakes her head. "Agatha and Septimus... their power is so great—it's... where would we even begin?"

"With you."

She looks at me, aghast. "Me? I wouldn't have a hope in..."

"You're Chosen," I interrupt her.

"So I've just recently found out," she grumbles, shaking her head. "Though I still don't know what to make of it."

"Make everything of it!" I insist. "Look what you did for me! Look what you did to the Priapen."

"Please, don't remind me."

But, I'm not going to allow her to continue feeling sorry for herself. Not when she needs to understand what she's capable of—what it means to be Chosen. "Tink, you're the only one powerful enough to stand a chance against their magic... and eventually defeat Morningstar—you and the other Chosen."

"The others maybe," she starts.

"It's your destiny," I interrupt.

"No!" she whispers, immediately standing up and then bolting from the room, knocking Quinn sideways as he enters.

"Ye really have a way with women," he clucks.

"I should say the same for you," I retort, standing up to stretch. I'm still weak, but I feel significantly better.

"Whit does that mean?"

"I think you know what it means," I answer, as I take a deep breath. "But we've got more important things to talk about right now."

"Such as?" Quinn asks.

I lean on him, since I'm not fully restored to myself. "Come. Let's go check on the situation up top."

ELEVEN
TINKER

Ensconcing myself in a corner of the deck amid some boxes, I close my eyes and try to push everything away. I can't deal with the things everyone expects of me. I'm just a small and inconsequential Fae and I've lived a very sheltered life since Zegar has been caring for me in Neverland. He's let no harm come to me and I've done little to grow my power here.

If anything, I've done everything I could to diminish it after what happened with my aunt. I can't be responsible for doing so much damage to anyone ever again. Granted, my uncle, Septimus, deserves to have his reign of terror brought to an abrupt end, but I'm not the one to do it. I can't bring myself to hurt anyone else and, even if I could, I lack what it would take to bring him down. Or Agatha, for that matter.

It's a death sentence to go up against them, not only for me, but for anyone who tries to help me. What happens if I fail and Septimus or Agatha goes after Peter, Quinn, or Zegar? How can I have that responsibility fall on my wings? I simply can't.

I'm lost in my own thoughts as I hear the boxes in front of me being pulled to one side, scraping across the deck, exposing me to Peter and Quinn, who stand there looking at me with an expression that conveys their sadness at my inability to be what they seem to think I should be.

I cower further into the corner, trying to shrink my tiny frame into an even smaller space, but it's no use.

"Why won't you leave me alone?" I whine.

"We cannae leave ye alone, lass," Quinn responds. "We need ye. We came a long way to find ye an' get ye out of this horrid place."

"I didn't ask you to come for me. Zegar and I were perfectly happy here alone."

"I don't think that's true," Peter reasons. "Perhaps you'd like it to be, but I don't think it really is."

"It doesn't matter. I don't want to be bothered with all this madness, all this violence and war and all this nonsense about Chosen ones."

"Tink, you can't just run away from this."

"It's not my responsibility, Peter," I reply.

"We don't have a prayer without you."

"I don't care," I say as I look up at him, my jaw tight.

"That cannae be true," Quinn says.

I won't look at him. I can't. Instead, I look down at my hands, at my tiny fingers which look so fragile and yet… yet they aren't fragile. My hands have carried out the will of my mind and done horrible things with my magic. I suddenly envy Prince Payne—he's able to sleep through all of this, to take shelter during the day, away from everyone. I wish I could do the same—lock myself away in some dark room to avoid the inquisition.

"I don't want this," I say softly.

"Tink, can we talk about it?" Peter asks.

"No," I answer as I look up at him, feeling on the verge of breaking down into a fit of tears. "Just please... go away."

He purses his lips for a moment and then smiles broadly, ignoring my own pained expression. Neither he nor Quinn speak for what feels like far too long. I squirm uncomfortably in their shadow, waiting for their admonishments of my cowardice to continue.

"What's going on here?" Zegar roars as he approaches from the opposite side of the deck and sees me all folded on myself behind the boxes. He appears to have found a stretch of fabric somewhere because the red cloth is now wrapped around his waist. He looks like some foreign genie from the deserts of Anoka come to grant me a wish. If he could, I would wish to never be part of this—to never be what I am—a murderer.

"They want me to do something I can't," I protest.

Zegar jerks his head angrily toward Quinn and Peter, demanding an explanation, so they oblige him. After they explain their side, Zegar sighs and reaches down for me, pulling me to my feet. Standing in front of me, he allows me to hide behind his bulky frame. I peek out from one side of him at Peter and Quinn, refusing to address them. I expect Zegar will send them away, but he doesn't. He merely gives me a place to feel safe, the thing he's always done best.

"I saw a flower growing out of a plank," Peter blurts out.

"What?" I ask.

"It was so many colors. Pink, blue, green, yellow, even gold. Such an odd combination, but beautiful. And there was a tiny little bug, so small you could hardly see him crawling along the door jamb. He looked at me. He had a face."

"A bug with a face?"

"Yes. He looked like Zegar when he's happy."

"Zegar is never happy," I reply, receiving only a grunt from the giant standing guard over me.

"Do you hear that, Zegar?" Peter asks the giant, who merely grunts. Then Peter looks back at me. "Sure Zegar is happy. When he looks at you he is," Peter says, drawing my attention back to him.

"I don't think I make him happy at all. I only frustrate him. He didn't ask to be signed up for guarding a useless faerie."

"You always make me happy," Zegar replies flatly, but doesn't offer anything further. Instead, he continues to stand guardian over me, or in front of me, as the case may be.

Peter lets it go and moves on to something else. He begins talking about his reflection instead. So self-centered. Of course, he has reason to be, but still. I puzzle at where he's going with all this disjointed nonsense.

"Do you know what makes me happy?" Peter asks,

but no one bothers answering. "I am beyond happy that I can see my pretty face in the glass of the ship's portal windows. I'm still handsome, thank the Gods above." Then he shrugs. "I've always been handsome, of course, but I was afraid that hellhound had taken my good looks from me forever! And when I was afraid that blasted creature had taken my looks from me, all I could wonder was how would I ever woo the fair maidens with a bedeviled face?"

"Peter," Quinn starts. "Now might nae be the best time…"

But Peter isn't listening. He's too busy listening to himself. "All the skin might have burned away, leaving me faceless altogether, and how would that be? Children would shriek in my presence. Their fathers would demand I wear a mask. I would become known only as the faceless man that walks among them."

I tilt my head to one side, still puzzling why he's rambling about such silly things, but he seems to just get more ridiculous as he goes on. It's almost comical how he jumps from one thing to the next, content to ramble on like an imbecile who can't complete a single sequence of thought. Now he's simply listing things that seem to have no common thread without any explanation of why.

"The sunshine, Zegar's bad cooking, Tink's quite shapely legs, a frog that turned unusual colors as it hopped along the deck, Prince Payne as he snores during the daytime and seems to be completely unaware of how useless he is, being chased by a hellhound and living to tell about it…"

"Whit are ye babblin' aboot?" Quinn asks.

"The hellhound melted his brain, clearly," Zegar interjects.

"I'm listing everything that's made me happy today," Peter answers with that broad grin of his. "It's a trick I've been using since I was a boy. It helps me get through the tough times. *Horde your happy thoughts like a dragon hordes gold and sift through them when you need it most.* That's what I'm doing. I'm sifting through my treasures."

"Why?" I ask.

He shrugs. "I've done a lot, hurt a lot of people. You though, Tink, you're different from me, from people like me. You are truly kind and you're worthy of so much more than you imagine. I can't just let you be crippled by self-doubt. It's not right at all. So, I'm trying to do everything I can to bring you out of this funk you're in and motivate you to know your own self worth."

I frown at him. "I told you about my aunt. I told you I killed her. I'm not worthy of anything. I've killed someone who didn't deserve it and for what reason?"

"That's where you are wrong," Peter starts, but Quinn interrupts.

"An accident doesnae make ye a bad person, Tink. Ye never intended to kill yer aunt—'twas Morningstar's influence that made ye do it. An' ye cannae blame yerself for that."

"It doesn't make you unworthy," Peter continues,

frowning at Quinn because he apparently didn't appreciate the conversation being hijacked. "It's just what it is: an accident that was never meant to happen."

"I can't take it back," I pout.

"No, but you can move on. You can do something else, something that will help the people who need you most."

"An', Tink," Quinn starts, pulling my attention to him. "There's somethin' Ah've been wantin' to tell ye, but Ah wasnae sure jist how to tell ye," he starts and then rubs the back of his neck and wears the expression of someone who's battling a conundrum.

"What?" I ask.

"Yer Aunt Saxe… she's nae exactly… dead."

"What do you mean, she's not exactly dead? I already told you I killed her! I saw it with my own eyes."

He shakes his head. "Aye, while that might be true, she's in a… somewhat alive," he starts, but then loses his train of thought as Peter takes over.

"A semi-animate state."

"What does that mean?"

"It means… she sort of looks like a ghost—as in she's a bit transparent, but she's sentient all the same. She's essentially as… alive as it's possible for her to be."

"How… how is that even possible?"

"Princess Briar Rose, one o' the Chosen that has recently emerged, has control over the dead," Quinn explains. "She's reanimated The Blue Faerie."

110

I frown at Quinn and then look at Payne, knowing he comes from Bloodstone Castle. "Is that true?"

"It is," he says. "I have seen the Blue Fairie with my own eyes."

I feel my mouth drop open. And I'm quiet for a few seconds. I notice Zegar says nothing and I wonder if he knew this all along, as well. "Why didn't you tell me?" I ask, facing all of them.

They both take a deep breath in unison. "We thought there should be a right place and time," Peter starts.

Quinn nods. "We werenae sure how ye would react, given the details ye told us 'bout her death, so we wanted to make certain the timing was right—that ye were ready to receive such information."

I don't know what to say to that—whether to be grateful to them that they waited to tell me or whether I should be angry. Instead, I just sit with the information for another few seconds before looking up at them. "Where is she?"

"Bloodstone Castle with Maura LeChance," Peter answers.

"The opposite direction of Sweetland," I say.

Quinn nods. "But that doesnae mean we cannae visit both," he says. "We could go from Sweetland to Bloodstone."

I shake my head. No matter what they say or do, they will never convince me I'm capable of destroying such an immense evil as Agatha and Septimus. "I can't do this, Peter. I can't defeat Septimus. Or Agatha, for

that matter. The scales are tipped in their favor. They
will win. Septimus, alone, is so much stronger than I
am and I don't have the time it would take to prepare to
go up against him."

"There you're wrong," Peter insists. "You are so
much more than you imagine."

Before I can respond, he steps toward me, cupping
my chin in his rough, but somehow gentle hands, and
kisses me with such passion, my wings flutter wildly,
sending pixie dust flying all around. Small flowers
spring up from the deck around us as he searches my
mouth with his, drinking me in until he's had his fill
and begins to pull away.

"I've wanted to do that for a very long time," Peter
says.

"Pan, you'll keep your hands to yourself from now
on," Zegar says, glaring at him, ever the loyal protector.

And Quinn looks unhappy, as well. In fact, his
cheeks are flushed and he refuses to look at either one
of us.

"I've heard stories about faeries like you, Tink,"
Peter continues. "I know you'll find a way to
understand what you are and what your destiny is. You
can do this—I know you can."

I try to protest, but he cuts me off with a second
kiss, leaving me gasping for air as he lets me go again.
His eyes are focused on mine in a heated gaze. He can
take me right here on the deck amid the flowers; Quinn
and Zegar can watch for all I care.

"You can do this," he repeats. "I know you will

find a way. All you need is a plan and I can help you carry it out. It's just that simple."

"And that complicated," I pout, my brow furrowed together in a little knot.

"I have all the faith in the world in you." He looks up at the others and nods. "We all do."

I smile at him, proud he believes in me so much. I feel empowered, brave, at least for a moment. But, as soon as those feelings fade, there's nothing but fear and self-doubt left remaining. How in the world can I hope to go up against Septimus and Agatha? How can I hope to go up against Morningstar?

The fear still lingers and I don't know how to make it go away so I can be half as brave as Peter seems to think I am.

You can only try, Tink, I tell myself.

And there's truth to that statement. I can fail and I probably will fail, but what am I really if I never even try?

It's right then and there that I make a decision: I'll do whatever I have to for Peter to be proud of me, for him to kiss me like that again.

Zegar steps away from us with a grunt, disappearing toward the front of the ship with Quinn close behind him. I wonder if Quinn is jealous of Peter kissing me or if he just wants to give us privacy? I hope Peter kisses me again, now that they've both gone, but he doesn't. Instead, he turns away, leaving me to gather my thoughts alone behind my boxes once again.

Except now, I don't want to be alone.

TWELVE
PETER

"The batmen are back," Quinn yells, running from where he'd been perched to keep watch.

"Are you kidding?"

"Ah wish Ah was. Whit can Ah say, but they're a real bastard to kill."

He barely finishes getting the words out of his mouth when one of the loathsome creatures drops down in front of me. I prepare myself for yet another fight, despite feeling the fatigue of my round with the hellhound. Even as I prepare myself for my opponent, I soon find him being swept sideways and over the nearby railing by the tail of Zegar, who has shifted to join the fight. His massive crocodile takes up a good portion of the ship's deck and he uses his immense shape to our advantage, simply knocking batmen off the sides and sending them downward to a watery grave.

I chuckle as I realize Zegar isn't even aware of the favor he's just done me—he'd simply entangled with another of the batmen and accidentally took down the one facing me. My amusement is short-lived as a third of the monstrosities drops down near the steering wheel by Tink. Quinn rushes toward her, when he's cut off by a fourth that sends him floundering overboard on the opposite side. Tink is off like a shot after him, leaving me to face her would be attacker.

And blasted Payne is still asleep below deck, the sun still high in the sky.

I'm about to lock in with the batman, when Tink comes shooting back over the bough, dropping a flailing Quinn onto the deck, and blasts a cloud of magic-filled-pixie dust that turns the batman to ash. What's left of him blows out into the air and disappears into the nothing. The ship speeds ahead, the sounds of bats screeching into the growing void around us, but growing fainter as we reach the edge of the world. I breathe a sigh of relief as we finally leave Neverland and continue on toward Delorood and then Sweetland.

"I don't know about the rest of you, but I could stand a break from all this fighting," I say, sighing. I've had a near brush with death, then a kiss with the very lovely faerie, and now another battle? I haven't even had time for supper. "How can there be so many of them? They're like roaches."

"Aye, that is bein' far too kind to them," Quinn replies, rubbing a dark mark on his jaw where one of them clipped him with what passed for a fist.

"They're in pain," Tinker says quietly.

"Pain?' Zegar replies, now shifted back to his giant human form, wrapping his nudity back up with the heavy piece of cloth he found in the storage racks down below.

"Yes," Tink insists. "Don't forget, they were once people before they became those monstrosities. They don't want to be what they are. They've been infected, enchanted to become the monsters we see, driven to violence. They don't want to do what they're summoned for, but they have no choice."

"How do ye know for sure?" Quinn asks. "Ah always believed that was jist a contrived story."

"One of them touched me and I could see snippets of his previous life when he was just a man. Now, he's that... thing."

"What did you get from him?" I ask her.

She shrugs. "Just that he doesn't know where his family is—or if they're alive or if they're like him now. There's no communication among the batmen, no sense of working together toward any common goal. Instead, they're led directly by Agatha. Her goal is their goal and they know nothing else."

"How horrifyin'," Quinn says.

"I can relate," I reply, still reeling from the feeling the hellhound created in me. There was a need to fight, but it was futile as more of its evil took me from the inside. If Tink hadn't saved me, I would have been consumed and lost all sense of myself. It had already been so difficult to even think about who I was or what I was supposed to be doing as the creature's power grew within me.

A sense of relief floods me as I look out into the quiet fog that's begun to dissipate from around us. We've moved up from the water and into the clouds, putting some distance between us and any batmen that might still appear from the depths. Things are quiet up here. It's a blessing to finally have some peace.

The feeling is short-lived as we find ourselves approaching another ship with the name *Siren's Song* emblazoned on its hull. It looks familiar, but I have a tough time placing it. Where have I encountered this ship before?

"What now? We're almost in Delorood—in friendly seas," Zegar scowls.

"I don't know. Let's first find out what that ship wants," I reply, watching the ship carefully as it approaches.

I don't have to wonder long. It's as if the ship propels itself forward at triple speed, one moment seeming small in the distance and the next, floating along right beside us.

"Jist two ships passin' in the night," Quinn jokes, but the smile falls from his face as more than a dozen men suddenly appear on the deck and propel themselves down upon us. Before we can blink, there are men everywhere—surrounding us. It's as if they've moved leaps and bounds in a mere blink. I don't understand how it's possible.

Before I can take another breath, the strangers have already seized everyone in their meaty paws.

"Let her go!" Zegar demands from over my shoulder.

I turn toward the sound of his gruff voice to find both he and Tink covered by large nets, but not just

your average fishing gear. These sparkle with some sort
of enchantment that keeps even someone as large as
Zegar from fighting free of them. I'm guessing the nets
prevent him from shifting, as well. Otherwise, he'd
already be ripping his way free of them.

"I can't use my magic," Tinker wails. "The ship
won't hold very long without it."

"Guess we better get this garbage off our deck fast,
Quinn," I say with a nod.

Almost in unison, we shove our attackers forward,
pulling long blades from our waists to face off against
the men surrounding us. Quinn and I fight back to back,
protecting one another from any rear assaults as we
struggle to keep the men at bay. Like the ship, itself, the
men look familiar, but I can't wrap my head around
where I've seen them before. As far as I can tell,
they're all human, though I can't account for the speed
with which they move.

"You're outnumbered, mate," one of them cackles,
not a tooth in his ugly head.

"We've dealt with worse than the likes of you
scallywags," I taunt him back.

"Then let's see who owns this vessel when our
blades are down. Mine will be in your chest," he slurs.

"You give yourself far too much credit, you
thieving scoundrel. You have no idea who you're
pirating today."

"Aye, 'tis that so? Then enlighten me."

"I'm Peter Pan and you're about to meet your
death."

There's a brief hesitation as the man seems to recognize my name, but the hesitation only lasts for a second before he settles right back into squaring off against me. Our blades meet and we dance about one another, each determined to be the end of the other. I begin slowly making my way toward the nets holding Tinker and Zegar, hoping to perhaps free them with a side swipe of my blade between thrusts at this motley fool in front of me.

It proves too much to hope for, as more of them drop onto the deck from the ship above, blocking any hope I have of getting to the nets without taking quite a few of them on. They continue to blip in and out of view, moving exquisitely fast.

Things escalate until there's nothing but a whirlwind of blades and bad intentions as we fight with our boarders, sending several of them to their graves. Still, we are outnumbered and with the speed at which they move, they will tire us out in no time. I'm not sure how many I can continue to stave off, but my concerns turn to something much more threatening as the thud of boots sounds from behind me.

"Ah want them alive," a familiar voice roars, but this time, it isn't just some vague thought in my head that I might know the man. No. I know exactly who that voice belongs to and it stops me dead in my tracks. My opponent's blade comes dangerously close to my heart as the man's sword intervenes, knocking it free of his hand.

"Ah said Ah wanted them alive!" he roars at the

man, who cowers back and drops his eyes, showing immediate obedience to the captain of his ship—but this isn't just any captain. This is the only captain who can strike bile into my throat. Both Quinn and I forget our fight, instead turning toward the new visitor.

"Hook," Quinn hisses at him.

"In the flesh," Hook replies with a dramatic wave of his metal appendage, smiling broadly as if he's greeting old friends. No wonder his men were able to move exceedingly fast—his ship must be enchanted, and thus, so is his crew.

The ship makes a sudden lilt toward the right, and Hook glances toward Tink and Zegar beneath their nets.

"Git her out o' that thing or we'll all drop to our deaths," he commands his men as he faces Tink again. "Dinnae get any ideas, my fair Fae or yer friends will pay the price. Jist keep this ship on the go while we all have ourselves a little discussion."

Tink is freed and guides the ship again downward into the water. The *Siren's Song* moves downward with us, settling into the dark waves by our side and dropping a gang plank from their deck to ours, but no one else boards. Instead, the men file back toward their own ship, leaving only Hook and a few of his men behind.

***

TINKER

121

Free of the net, I have no intention of just letting Captain Hook take our ship—oh, I've heard plenty of stories about him and none of them good. I move down to the water to free up as much of my power as I can and watch as many of Hook's men disembark from our ship. Once they're clear, I charge everything that isn't nailed down to do my bidding. A rope shoots out from one side, grabbing one of the remaining pirates by the leg and yanking him sideways so he hits the deck with a loud thud.

Hook jerks his head in the direction of the noise as a group of buckets, brooms, deck brushes and the like hover above his head, taking aim at him. He glances up at them and then back at me with a smirk I find most unsettling.

"I'm not going to let you hurt anyone on this ship," I tell him, summoning all my courage.

"Aye, 'tis good. Ah didnae come here to hurt anyone on the ship, me wee lass."

"I'm not your wee lass!" I yell back at him, folding my arms against my chest in a huff. "And I don't believe you."

"Aye, ye should."

"And why is that?"

His smile is handsome. Ahem, really handsome. He definitely reminds me of Quinn, only an older and hardened version. Whereas Quinn has a certain shyness to him, Hook is all brazen smiles and confident familiarity.

"Ah'm really a likeable chap once ye get to know me," he replies, taking a step forward as the buckets follow, clanging together.

"Stop walking," I demand, my heart feeling like it might explode as it thuds mightily against my chest.

Hook stops and looks at me, letting out a loud sigh and shrugging his shoulders. "'Tis jist a misunderstanding."

"A misunderstanding?" I demand. I know all about pirates from Zegar's stories—and I know enough to know they can't be trusted.

"Aye, ye're flyin' Agatha's colors," Hook continues with another shrug. "We thought ye were a fleet o' her soldiers. They're a violent bunch, that lot." I glance up at our flag and then back at him, sizing him up again. Is he a liar or was that really the reason why he attacked us?

"We're not soldiers for Agatha."

"Ah can see that now. Like Ah said, 'twas a mistake. Agatha's been threatenin' us with violent action fer quite some time, so it's nae wonder we attacked ye." He pauses for a moment and then narrows his eyes at me. "Boot why would ye fly her colors?"

"I hadn't noticed they were her colors," I answer as I glance up at the masts overhead. "I salvaged this ship from the shores of our island and rebuilt it, but I never thought to take down the flag."

"Or mayhap ye thought it might keep ye from being noticed by her men if ye were flyin' the same flag they were?"

"Perhaps," I tell him, more willing to let him think I'm that cunning than to admit I just hadn't thought to remove it. I turn my attention back to him instead of my befuddled thoughts. "Why should I believe you?"

"'Tis a fair question. In yer shoes, Ah dinnae suppose Ah would believe me either," he replies before looking past me, toward Quinn. He takes a deep breath, and it's then that I realize he's been chatting it up with me because he's... nervous to face his brother. I can see as much in his gaze.

"Quinn, please put yer weapons down. Ah've come as yer ally." Quinn doesn't answer, and there's a long moment of uncomfortable silence. Hook then interrupts it. "We've nae seen each other in sooch a long time, brother."

"Ah'm nae yer brother," Quinn replies through gritted teeth, nearly spitting the words.

"Och, come now. Cannae we let bygones be bygones?"

Quinn narrows his eyes on Hook. "Is that what you call what you did to me? A bygone?"

"Nae, boot Ah cannae change the past now, nae matter how badly Ah wish Ah could," Hook answers and there's something in his voice that speaks to the pain inside him. That, or he's just a good actor. I'm actually not sure which.

Quinn doesn't appear convinced. "Ah dinnae have time for yer games, Hook. We are on our way to Sweetland an' from there, Bloodstone Castle."

"Bloodstone Castle?" Hook repeats. "For whit

purpose?"

"Tinker needs to see the Blue Faerie."

Suddenly I'm reminded my Aunt Saxe is somewhat alive and everything above Hook's head drops, hitting him on the head and shoulders. He curses loudly, scowling at me.

"Why did ye do that?"

"I didn't mean to. I lost my focus," I reply unapologetically with a shrug. News of my Aunt Saxe will take some getting used to and I'm still not sure how I feel about seeing her again. Of course, I have to—there's no way around that. And I want to… I'm just not sure what I would say, how I would start the conversation.

I'm sorry I set you on fire?

No, that doesn't sound right. Furthermore, I'm not even sure if she'd want to see me. For all I know, she detests me. And I wouldn't blame her at all if such was the case.

Hook smiles at his brother, pulling my attention back to the conversation at hand. "As Ah said, we thought ye were one o' Agatha's ships."

"Regardless," Quinn answers. "We need to eventually get Tinker to the Blue Faerie."

I glance back at Hook and then turn toward Quinn and Peter once more, noting how both of them continue to stare at Hook, their expressions far less than friendly. I glance toward Zegar, who is still fuming beneath the net they've cast over him.

"Let Zegar out of that thing," I tell Hook.

Hook doesn't make any move to do anything, but just studies Zegar. "Ah dinnae know. That doesnae seem like a fantastic idea to me." Then he waves his hand at me. "How do ye think Ah got this hook in the first place?"

"I wouldn't know."

"Well, yer buddy, Pan there, saw fit to cut off me hand an' that monstrosity ate it 'afore Ah could retrieve it. So, Ah ended up with this bloody thing instead," he says, holding up the hook again.

"He's not a monstrosity, and if you don't release him, you'll regret it," I demand. "You'll lose more than a hand."

Hook smiles broadly at me again and I definitely get the feeling he's a ladies man and then some. He just has a smooth swagger to him that almost bests Peter's own self-confident arrogance. "Ah think Ah might regret lettin' him out even more."

"He's not going to do you any harm," I reply, turning toward Zegar. "Are you?"

Zegar doesn't reply.

"Are you, Zegar?" I repeat.

"Yes, I am!" Zegar finally responds. "I'm going to take a lot more than his hand if I'm given the chance!"

"Ah rest my case," Hook replies with a wave of his good hand.

"Zegar," I say, breathing in deeply because I don't have the time for this or the interest. "I need you to behave. No one is going to hurt anyone. Got it?"

Zegar grunts and looks away, stubborn to a fault.

126

"Zegar!" I bark at him.

"Fine," he responds as he looks at me again, jaw and lips tight. "Only because you asked me, but I can't promise the situation won't change if Hook crosses me."

I look at the man in question. "He won't."

"Ah won't?" Hook replies with a big smile, but drops the smile once he sees my scowl. Then he nods. "Right. Nae. Ah willnae cross ye, Zegar, nor any o' the lot o' ye."

"A truce then," I say, deciding it's the best I can hope for, if it's even possible. I hope it's possible because it appears, for the time being anyway, that Hook and the rest of us are on the same side. If he can be trusted, that is. And that's a very big 'if'.

"A truce," Hook replies. I turn to Zegar, and he nods. Hook motions toward one of his men and they pull away the net, watching with a bit of awe as Zegar rises to his full height, all ten feet of him. They glance uncertainly at Hook and he nods at them, motioning toward their own boat.

"Back to the ship. Ye're done here, crew," he tells them. Then he faces me again. "Where to, lass? Are ye stayin' in Delorood on yer way to Sweetland an' then the Blue Fairie?"

That's a good question and I turn to the others. "Peter? Quinn? Can we rest in Delorood just for a bit?" We're all exhausted and I can't remember the last time I had a proper meal.

"Ah dinnae like it," Quinn says, shaking his head.

127

He's speaking to me, but his eyes are still on Hook.

"Me neither," Peter adds, his gaze on mine, searing through my skin with his heat.

"Please?"

Quinn groans and Peter sighs, both shrugging their shoulders in defeat.

"If that's what you really want, Tink," Peter answers.

"It is."

"Great," Hook answers as he claps his hands together and gives us all another big grin that no one reciprocates. "Then let's get on our way, shall we? Ah'll lead ye to Drowning Cove. Jist follow me," he finishes, sounding quite jovial.

"That's the last thing Ah want to do," Quinn growls at him.

"We'll be right behind you," I respond, watching as Hook returns to his ship and disappears below the railings onto his own deck.

"I don't like this," Peter says.

"We can use his help, and the Drowning Cove is only just a stop off along the way," I inform him. "Don't let whatever happened in the past cloud your judgement," I continue. "For all intents and purposes, it seems we're all on the same side."

"That's easy for ye to say. Ye werenae the one he..." Quinn begins to say, but he stops and abruptly walks away, as though he can't even allow the words to come from his mouth.

I turn toward Peter, and he shrugs again.

"He'll be fine," he says, following me to the helm of the ship as we make our way forward in the dark waters, now accompanied by the *Siren's Song*.

THIRTEEN
TINKER

"Tinker, this is Aria," Hook tells me as we exit the ship in Delorood and make our way across the slippery black rocks along the shore to what looks like a cave. Inside, the cave is much taller and longer than how it appears from the outside. It sits to one side of what appears to be a castle, embedded into the rocks below. The cave leads into one of several entrances to the upper towers and dungeons below the water that surrounds the entire complex.

Because it's still daylight, we opt to leave Prince Payne in his sleeping quarters, below deck. Once night is upon us, he'll find his way out.

"It's good to meet you, Tinker," Aria purrs.

I'm instantly jealous of her because I've never seen such a beautiful woman, er mermaid. She's all sex and desire, tall and slender with a generous bosom and perfectly shaped rear. I could never look so long and lean with my tiny stature and I'm suddenly self-conscious.

Aria's voice sounds like music, but unlike other sirens, she doesn't lure sailors in with it. Actually, none of the sirens lead human men to their doom any longer.

130

They stopped drowning sailors ages ago. Instead, they guard Aria, protecting her when she comes to meet with the men who flock here to be graced with her attentions.

"Hook," she says with a smile that reeks of intimacy between the two of them. "Is Bastion with you?"

"Aye, he'll be along once the ship is shored oop."

Her demeanor goes from friendly to cool in a manner of seconds. It takes a moment for me to realize she's not looking at me with her harsh stare, but past me at someone approaching from behind. I turn to see Peter and Quinn.

"What is *he* doing here?" she demands, her tone suddenly sharp.

"Hello, Aria," Peter replies with a sheepish grin.

"You're not welcome here, Pan," she answers as she turns to face Hook. "Why would you bring him here? Have you forgotten what he did to you?"

Hook holds up his arm, letting the light send glints off the metal to reflect against the crystal walls in the mouth of the mammoth cave. "Be a bit hard to forget that, wouldn't it, me dear? Ah've moved on though. At least moved on past the whole bit aboot Pan cuttin' me hand off. Now, lettin' that scaled freak eat it—well, that's still a sore spot."

"Regardless, I haven't forgiven him for maiming you," Aria says as she continues to glare daggers at Peter, who continues to smile at her.

"All is fair in war, m'lady," Peter says with a

shrug.

"Aye, 'tis true enough," Hook says with a nod.

"I don't want to see him," Aria says, turning her back on Peter. "See Pan and Quinn to their quarters," she barks at one of her nearby servants. Then she faces me and her features soften. "Tinker, would you be so kind as to assist me?"

Aria then takes my hand and pulls me into the cave, walking me to a nearby door that leads into a quite brilliant sitting room.

I marvel at the shimmering gems and smooth black slate that makes up the walls. A nearby fireplace is fashioned completely with large seashells, something that's also been used to furnish the room. Of course, I wonder why a mermaid would have use of a fireplace, but there it is. I suppose she gets just as cold as humans do on the land.

She offers me a seat in an oversized clam shell sitting on a base of water stones and filled with plush cushions to make it more comfortable. Other pieces of furniture are made of faceted silver that sparkles, sending off beams of light like one of the mirrored balls used in gardens.

"This place is lovely," I marvel, still gawking at the colors that are cast all around by the hammered silver and crystals hitting the gems embedded in the walls. It's not what you expect from a cave at all, though I suppose this is technically not just a cave, but part of the castle above.

"Thank you. It's more of a work location than

home, but we try to keep it cozy for our visitors."

"So, you don't live here?"

"Oh, heavens no," Aria answers with a bell laugh. "It's much too small." Then she quiets as she looks at me and appears to study me for a few seconds. "Enough about such silly topics. Tell me what's led you to keeping such questionable company."

"Who? Hook?"

She laughs again and waves a long and delicate hand in the air. "No, of course not Hook. I'm talking about Peter Pan and his Lost Boy, Quinn."

Instantly, I feel myself coloring and I have to remind myself not to be offended. We're on the same side as Hook and Aria and it's becoming quite clear that we have to put our differences aside. "Peter and Quinn have actually been a huge help to me and I wouldn't call them 'questionable company' at all. In fact, I've heard tales of them for as long as I can recall."

"Tales?"

I nod. "Zegar knows all about Peter Pan and the Lost Boys."

"Zegar?" she repeats and her jaw goes tight again as I realize this whole friendship thing between us might be a harder sell than I previously thought. "That giant crocodile bastard is with you, too?"

I swallow hard and remind myself not to turn this into an argument. Aria doesn't know Pan, Quinn and Zegar yet, so she doesn't know how caring and kind they can be. All she does know is that Pan and Zegar are responsible for her lover's lost appendage, so she understandably dislikes them. "Yes. Zegar's keeping an eye on our ship. He didn't fancy coming up just yet. And, um, Prince Payne is with us too—but he's asleep since the sun is still high in the sky."

She doesn't react to the news of Prince Payne, so I figure she either doesn't know him or isn't concerned with him.

"They are good guys, Aria," I insist, wanting and needing to convince her of exactly that fact. If we're to be allies, we need to trust each other. "All of them. Peter, Quinn, and Zegar."

"I see." She doesn't sound convinced.

"We're all on the same side, fighting for the same thing," I say softly.

"I know."

"And if we're to be allies, we must act like allies."

She clears her throat and is quiet for a few seconds. Then her hard expression falls and she nods. "I suppose that's true."

"It is true," I say with certainty.

She nods again, but her mind is clearly elsewhere, because her eyes haze over. "Are they all your lovers, then?"

I laugh at the thought. "Good Gods, no!"

"Oh," she says and leans back into her chair, seeming confused. "The way they regard you and the way you regard them… it seemed you were."

"Well, it's complicated," I start.

"Are you lovers with the croc?" she continues.

134

"Zegar? No, he's like a brother to me," I admit. "He's been my guardian and protector since my Aunt Saxe left me on the island."

"And what of Pan and Hook's brother?"

"Well, I've only just met them—Quinn and Peter." At the mention of them both, I decide I'd rather be around my men. "I'm not sure how long I should leave Peter and Quinn out there with Hook. He and Quinn aren't exactly best mates."

"I'm sure they aren't," Aria agrees with a quick nod. "Family stuff. I've learned to never get involved in such squabbles. Always ends up a disaster." Then she smiles more broadly. "They'll be fine. Besides, they should be off to their quarters by now." She reaches out and takes my hand and there's something about her that's so warm—surprising considering she's essentially an enchanted fish. "Let's talk a bit more."

"About what?"

"About you staying for longer than just an introduction and then sailing off again. Surely, you're sea lagged and need a respite."

"I suppose we all do, but the nature of our quest is an important one."

"And what is that?"

"We are headed to Sweetland to reverse the disease Agatha has put on the people there. She's turned them into hellhounds and batmen."

Aria nods. "I had heard of this plague."

"Right. Then we are headed to Bloodstone Castle..." And my Aunt Saxe, I want to add, but I don't. I'm still not sure how I feel about this whole subject—Maura LeChance doesn't bother me, of course. But, I'm nervous about seeing my aunt again. I wonder if she hates me?

"Then stay for as long as you can," Aria says and claps her hands together as if I've already agreed. It seems she's in sore need of female company. "Let Quinn and Hook work out their differences and let everyone else get some well-deserved rest."

"Maybe it wouldn't hurt," I say as the thought of resting does definitely appeal…

She nods conspiratorially and gives me a smile. "I would love to see Hook and Quinn act like the brothers they were born to be."

I shrug. "I'm not sure that's possible."

"Everything is possible, Princess Tinker," Aria insists. "And Hook has desired nothing more than to be close to his brother."

"I have to admit, Hook is nothing like I imagined him to be. I mean, he's nothing like the stories Zegar has told me about him."

"Well, that just goes to show that you can't always trust the words of others. Sometimes, you have to see for yourself what the truth is."

I nod. "I guess so."

"Regardless, Quinn is the only family Hook has. And Hook wants to make things right with him… more than anything. It's all he talks about."

"And Peter?"

"That, I'm not so sure about," she answers.

"Neither of us have any love lost for Peter, but he comes as a package deal with Quinn and with you, doesn't he?"

I nod. "He does."

"Then, we'll just have to try to make what peace we can with Peter in order to further the cause."

"I understand and I appreciate the honesty—and the help." I stand up and start for the door. "I should go tell them I plan to extend our stay and maybe I can find a bed somewhere. I'm exhausted—we all are."

"I will certainly allow you to handle that first part. I doubt Peter and Quinn or Zegar want to share company with me right now, and I'm sorry to say the feeling is mutual. As for the bed, I can help you with that. I'll have a servant show you to your quarters and we shall meet again soon."

"Okay," I say with a smile. "Thank you again," I say as she waves a servant over and I follow them across the massive entrance of the cave to another door. Stepping inside, I find Peter pacing anxiously as he waits for me to arrive.

"Well?" Peter implores. "When are we leaving?"

FOURTEEN
QUINN

"Will ye sit down with me an' talk things out?"
Hook offers.

I eye him suspiciously as anger colors my mood.
I'll never forget what he's done to me, nor the hatred
that burns in my gut just from looking at the bastard.
What could we possibly have to discuss? He sold me to
horrible people who did unspeakable things to me and
landed me on an island with the other Lost Boys who
were doomed to live as children with only glints of gray
memories as to who they once had been.

"We've naethin' to say to one another."

"O' course we do," Hook insists. "We've each
been on different journeys for quite a while now an',
ye've saddled yourself with the likes o' Peter Pan."

I glare at him, the anger within me growing.
Perhaps it was too much to expect an apology from the
walloper, but I'd expected one, all the same. "Is that
whit ye want, then? Ye want to castigate me for takin'
up with Peter Pan?"

"Nae, Ah dinnae want to do that. Whit's done is
done. Pan is nae longer any threat to me."

"If ye think that, then ye've indeed changed, but

Ah'm nae sure it's fer yer better ends. Peter would slice ye open like a ripe melon, given half a chance."

"Ah dinnae think he would."

I glare at him further. His cocksureness is mind-blowing. "Whit makes ye say that?"

Hook shrugs. "Ye wouldnae let him."

"Ye think Ah wouldnae let him?" I laugh.

He nods. "Nae matter what grievances ye may have 'gainst me, we're still brothers."

"*Half-brothers* an' ye think too much o' yerself. Ah wouldnae care a damn if Pan slit ye from chin to navel."

"Brothers enough," Hook says and holds his chin in a stubborn set. "An' though ye say as mooch, Ah still dinnae believe ye."

"Regardless, Ah'm nae in the mood for talkin'."

"Whit are ye in the mood for then, lad?"

"Fightin'," I answer, wanting nothing more than to feel his face beneath my fists. "Ye feel oop to a bit o' battle?"

Hook chuckles. "Ye want to fight me? Fer whit purpose?"

"Ah owe ye an ass kickin'."

"An' ye think ye can accomplish that?"

"Ah do. Ye're nae match for me with yer one good hand."

"Ye think nae, huh? Okay, well let's do battle then an' we shall see, boot only on one condition."

"Whit condition would that be?" I nearly spit at him.

139

"If Ah win, then we sit down an' talk, man to man. Despite those boyish looks o' yours, ye are a man, are ye not?"

I glare at him. "That, Ah am."

He nods succinctly. "Nae rules then?"

"Nae rules."

"One rule."

I frown and breathe out a hearty sigh. "Bloody hell. Can ye nae even afford me a simple fight without tryin' to sway it in yer favor somehow?"

"Nae weapons," Hook says.

"Nae weapons?"

He nods. "Surely ye dinnae think me havin' one hand an' nae weapon is somehow to me advantage?"

"Yer missin' hand is more a weapon than the one Ah was born with. 'Tis hardly a disadvantage—ye havin' a hook."

Much to my surprise, he holds up the hook and pushes a button, expelling it so it loosens, allowing him to pull it free from its base. He lays the hook on the ground and holds up his stumpy appendage with only the base of the hooked attachment still present.

I nod. "Fine. Let's do this then."

"Good, let's fight this silly battle o' yours an' then we can settle other matters once Ah'm done with—"

I don't wait for him to finish. Instead, I charge forward, catch him around the middle, and push him as hard as I'm able. He flies backwards, losing his footing on the rocks and rolling sideways, as I leap atop him and he shoves me away from him with one hand. He could easily have clapped me soundly with the base that remained of his fake appendage if he'd wanted to. The wooden stump isn't as dangerous as a metal hook, but it could still pack a wallop with its weight. Still he doesn't attempt such a move.

"Dinnae be a big girl's blouse aboot it. Fight like a bloody man!" I bark at him, hopping to my feet, and squaring off against him again. If he's going easy on me, that will just further enrage me.

He doesn't respond, instead he launches himself forward, but misses as I side-step him with a loud laugh, taunting him. A group of sirens gather nearby to watch, giggling as I make him look like the fool he is. His face grows red with anger as he charges me again, sending me backwards toward the water. We fight, fist to fist, both weaponless as agreed upon.

"Quinn, ye moost know somethin'," he starts.

"Ah moost know whit?"

"Ah never sold ye into slavery," he insists.

"That's a load o' shite, thick an' steamin'."

He shakes his head. "While ye believed Ah was sellin' ye, the truth was Ah was bein' keelhauled by the ship's cap'n… so Ah wouldnae interfere with his plans for ye. While Ah was fightin' fer me life, tied to a line looped beneath the ship an' dragged under the ship's keel, Ah didnae know whit was happenin' to ye or Ah would have stopped it."

I'm quiet because I've never heard this explanation before—not that I've ever given Hook the chance to explain.

"If ye think for a second Ah would have willingly sold ye into such a miserable fate, ye never knew me at all, Quinn."

"When it happened, Ah was shocked ye allowed it to happen."

"Because Ah didnae allow it to happen! Ah didnae know it was happenin', nor would Ah ever have allowed it!"

All this time, I'd just assumed because he wasn't there, that he didn't care. And Peter had done nothing to try to prove Hook's innocence. His hatred for Hook had always reinforced my insecurity that my brother had sold me into such a horrible life. But, maybe such wasn't the case?

"Quinn, ye moost believe me. Ah'm nae fibbin' to ye," Hook insists. He might be many things, but a liar was never one of them. Perhaps.

My foot slips on the edge of the slick pebbles at the waterline and I fall into the ocean. I expect him to back off, content to have returned the favor of humiliation, but he comes for me in the water, heaving blow on blow against me. Some blows I block and some land with a sickening wet thud as we pound one another unrelentingly.

And I love every minute of it. How many times have I dreamt about pummeling Hook's fucking face in? How many times have I yearned for this exact moment? Countless times.

"Ah dinnae want to listen to yer stories o' woe an' shite," I say, though my tone isn't quite as angry as it was.

He deals me a hard blow that leaves my ear ringing as the hard base against his stump finally makes contact with me. He looks startled, perhaps not meaning to have used it against me. Still, it angers me that much more and I settle into a rapid fire series of punches to his belly. They land hard, the water not slowing them in the least.

He doubles over then, and I take pause. Have I really hurt him? I hope so and I don't hope so. My hatred for him continues to burn anew and yet, there's something else there, too. Much though I hate to admit it, we *are* brothers. We are blood. And maybe his story… maybe his story is true?

"Are ye fit to continue?" I ask as I roll over and get to my feet.

"Aye, but Ah dinnae know why we're botherin'. This resolves naethin' between us."

"Ye want to stop then?"

"Do ye?" he asks, still sitting in the surf.

A sigh escapes me as I ponder why I've started this fight in the first place. I think I just needed to get my aggression toward him out of my system, but how did I expect it all to end? Did I suppose we would fight to the death? No. Did I want to pull his arm up behind his back and make him cry Uncle? Perhaps.

"Aye, we'll call it a draw an' be done with it," I say, but I don't offer him an arm up. Instead, I just stand there, glaring at him.

"An' me explanation for the truth in whit happened

so long ago?"

I breathe out an exasperated sigh. I need to think, need to try to remember what happened all those years ago, need to ask myself if there's a chance his explanation could really be the truth. "Ah understand whit happened an' why, but I'm nae ready to forgive ye. The best I can offer is to work with ye to fight the evil that is Morningstar an' his ilk."

"Ah can live with that… for now," he replies, holding up his arm with the stump. I hesitated a moment before reaching forward, gripping his forearm and yanking him hard to his feet. He stands there a moment or so, before trying to pull me into a hug.

I suffer his affection as he pulls back and pats me on the back as though we're old friends, as though I don't hate him.

"Ah love ye, brother," he says. "Ah always have an' nae matter whit, Ah always will. Ah hope ye can see past yer anger an' consider what Ah've said. Ah hope ye can see the truth eventually."

And it's at that point that I decide I've had enough. My anger spikes, and I want nothing more than to be away from him. "Sure," I reply, trudging out of the water and letting myself drip dry on the rocks as the sirens gather around me to flirt and giggle. I enjoy their attention for a bit as I regroup and take stock of my injuries, which are numerous, but I can't say I feel them. I turn down their offers of more private attention, instead making my way to the room Peter and I have been directed to before I came out to confront Hook.

***

"Hello, Quinn," Peter says with a grin as I enter.

I squint at him, where he sits beside Tink on the bed, and wonder what they've been doing in my absence. I have a good idea and I'm not sure how I feel about it. I have no claim to Tink and yet I think of her as mine somehow. Still, I've not overlooked how she looks at Peter, even now, with me standing in front of her.

"What's goin' on in here?" I ask, noting that they definitely look as if they've been up to something, but it doesn't seem to be sexual in nature. Instead, I get a sense they've been plotting in my absence.

"We've been waiting on you," Tink says as she narrows her eyes at my battered face and body and then stands, immediately approaching me.

"Aye? Whit for? Were the two of you in need of my caustic wit an' scintillating conversation?"

"Quinn," she starts, reaching for my face which is, no doubt, pummeled something terrible.

"Always, but that's not why we were waiting for you," Peter replies. "What trouble did you find yourself in, old chap?" he finishes with a laugh.

"Whit then?" I demand, pushing Tink away because I'm not in the mood for her concern at the moment. My head is aching and I can't stop thinking about the things Hook said earlier. And in thinking about them, I can't stop wondering if they're true.

"We have a… proposition for you," Tink replies.

***
TINKER

"Quinn, your face!" I say as I force him to face me. I can tell he doesn't want me to fuss over him, but I don't care. His lip is split and bleeding all over the front of him, one eye is sealed shut and swollen, his cheek beneath it already turning black and blue and he's soaking wet. "What's happened to you?"

"*Hook* happened to me," Quinn responds.

Peter stands up then. "I'll punch him into the ground."

Quinn looks at Peter. "Too late—Ah've taken care o' him jist as he took care o' me."

"Then," I start, nervously chewing my lower lip. "Are we no longer welcome here?" I figure if it's come to blows between Hook and Quinn, Aria will probably want us on our way.

Quinn shakes his head. "Nae, 'twas a long time comin' between me brother an' me."

"I hope you walloped him until he can no longer stand, the son of a whore," Peter starts, but Quinn just looks at him and shakes his head. Then he takes a deep breath.

"Enough said oan the subject." He faces me again, lifting his eyebrows as best he can, but one won't move, owing to the swelling. "Whit's this proposition

146

o' yers, lass?"

I hold up my hands and touch his face as I close my eyes and channel my magic into him, just as I did to save Peter when he was in danger from the hellhound. Now that I know I can curb my magic and force it to heal, I feel confident and Quinn apparently agrees, because he allows me to tend to him.

"You're doing it, Tink," Peter whispers. I don't open my eyes, instead I continue to concentrate on healing Quinn. When I feel the time is right, I step back and open my eyes and find him much better off—his lip is mostly healed, the swelling around his eye and cheek is gone and he can open his eye again. The bruise is still there, but only slightly.

"Thank ye, lass," Quinn says and nods to me. I nod back at him and give him a smile. Then I turn to the subject I've been considering.

"I've been thinking about Briar Rose and what she does," I begin.

"Ye plan to reanimate the dead?" Quinn asks.

"No," I respond and look at him with an expression that begs him not to interrupt me with silly questions. "I don't have that sort of power. At least, I don't think I do..."

"Yer point, lass?" Quinn asks, and I can tell he's still short-tempered from his altercation with Hook. Whatever happened between the two of them was a long time coming and though I think it was probably necessary, I can't tell if it was enough for Quinn. He's hard to read at the best of times, but now, he's near impossible.

"Briar Rose uses her power to bring the dead into being, into becoming animated again. She shares her power with them and they are able to further fuel her death magic."

"Ah still dinnae understand," he says with a frown.

"I think I can keep my powers a bit steadier if I bond them," I explain. "If I share them so they exist outside of just myself."

Quinn stands there, looking from me to Peter, with a continued look of confusion. "Bond yer powers?" he finally replies.

"Yes. Briar did it with blood, but I think I need a bit more than that because I'm Fae. I think a mixture of blood and my own magic might do the trick."

"Whose blood?"

"Yours. Well, yours and Peter's. I want to bond the three of us together so we can share our power."

"We dinnae have any power."

"You do—your life force is exceptionally strong, Quinn. Yours and Peter's. I'm pretty certain I can draw on your strength and you can draw on my power. Together, we would all become stronger."

"Ah see, but Ah'm still nae sure Ah fully understand. How do ye propose to bond with Peter an' me?"

I pull free the small silver and glass vial I'd filled with my blood earlier. The light catches the glass, sending shimmering trails of gold across the walls around us. The magic mixes within it, sparkling vividly, casting bright hues into the mix. He and Peter marvel at it, watching it for a bit before refocusing on me.

"Whit is it?" Quinn asks, seemingly still somewhat mesmerized by the colors spinning around the room.

"It's my blood."

"That's blood?" Quinn and Peter ask, almost in perfect unison.

"Yes. *My* blood."

"It's beautiful," Quinn gasps.

"Thank you," I say proudly, not sure why having my blood complimented pleases me so much, but it does, all the same.

"What are we supposed to do with it?" Peter asks. "You don't want us to drink it or something disgusting like that, do you?"

"Drink it? No. Of course not. Do you take me for a vampire?" I joke. Speaking of, Payne should be mobile soon, as the sun is starting to set.

"Then whit?" Quinn asks. Yes, he's certainly shorter now than he normally is. Whatever happened with Hook has clearly bothered him and it's on his mind still.

"Back before the Seelie Court was destroyed, they made guild tattoos with faerie blood, sealing a bit of our magic into the tattoos for protection. If I tattoo each of you with my blood and then tattoo myself with yours, I think I can establish a link between us, making all of us bonded."

"That doesnae sound so bad," Quinn replies, still

watching the colors that are now filling the air around us like some sort of psychedelic lighting show.

"Well, there's more," I tell him, feeling the heat rise through my cheeks as I continue with the rest—the parts they still need to know and understand before they agree to anything. It's enthralling to think about, but a bit embarrassing to say to both of them, standing there together, looking at me expectantly.

"Tell us," Quinn coaxes.

"If we want the bond to be as strong as it possibly can be, we'll need to add something else to it."

"Something else?" Quinn asks.

I nod and clear my throat, feeling my cheeks going hot. "Yes, we'll need to seal our bond further... with *something else*."

"You keep saying that. What *something else*?" Peter asks.

Might as well just spit it out, I tell myself. *There's no use in beating around the bush.*

"An act of love, peace, creation. Light and love are the marks of the Seelie Fae. Those who deserve our affection get it in spades and I believe... I believe the two of you deserve mine."

"That is no small offer," Peter says.

I nod as I look at him. "I've heard so much about the two of you from Zegar that I felt like I knew you long before you arrived in Neverland. I mean, I've idolized you and sometimes when you meet the person you've been idolizing, it can be a disappointment, but not with the two of you. You're everything Zegar said you were—and more. I mean, I know you might not feel the same for me…"

"You're not the only one who has heard tales, Tink," Peter's quick to respond. "Quinn and I have been told many times of a beautiful faerie princess who was lost on a horrible isle. And this lovely princess was kind and sweet…"

"Aye, an' with a stubborn streak a mile wide," Quinn adds with a chuckle.

I smile at him as Peter continues. "But none of those stories hold a candle to the reality of you. You don't seem to know just how incredible you are. You are magical in a way that has nothing to do with being Fae."

Quinn nods his agreement, and his eyes are focused on me. There's something in them—something burning and fiery in their depths. And that something lifts my heart. It's affection and, as I look at him, then at Peter, I realize the same affection I feel for them, they feel for me.

"I would be honored to be bonded to the two of you," I say in a small voice.

"Do ye think this can really work?" Quinn asks.

"I don't know, but it's the only way I can think of that might give us an edge, that might give us enough power for the battles that lie ahead. I know you think it's just self-doubt on my part, but I truly don't think I'm strong enough to take on my uncle Septimus. He's so much more powerful than I am, and he's been honing his skills for far longer. Not to mention the fact that he's got an ally in Agatha. While he's been busy training and growing his power, I've been tucked away on an island, afraid to even use mine."

"But you are strong, Tink," Peter insists. "We've seen your power."

"You've seen me make an oasis to get away from the bleak existence of the island. You've seen me power a ship. And you've seen me… dispatch a Priapen. Those things are nothing compared to what Septimus is capable of doing."

"We've also seen ye use yer power to cage a hellhound inside Peter's mind."

"I'm not complaining and I'm proud of the things I've done, but… I know it's still not enough. Yet, with both of you added to the mix, I think it would be… potentially." I take a deep breath and face them both. "Are you willing to join with me and become a singular force against the evil Agatha and Septimus have unleashed?"

"Ah cannae recall havin' ever wanted anythin' as much as Ah want ye since Ah first left Neverland," Quinn replies in a soft voice.

"I agree, wholeheartedly," Peter adds, with none of his robust playfulness. They're both serious and the way they look at me shows me just how much they care for me.

"Perhaps we'd better get started then," I say, my heart racing with excitement.

FIFTEEN
PETER

"What do we do?" I ask, eager to get on with this bonding ritual. It's hard to say if I'm more excited about having the faerie power the tattoo will bring, or just excited to finally get my chance with Tinker. I'm okay with sharing her with Quinn. We're used to sharing everything anyway and we have our own love between us, not romantic, of course, but devoted in a way that only those who have suffered greatly with one another can understand.

Tink hesitates. "First… you should know you might… end up being able to use some of my powers if we link ourselves together so intimately."

"Really?" Quinn asks, all smiles. Apparently he has made his peace with sharing her, just as I have.

"Yes," she replies, fetching a needle and lighting a candle to heat the tip. We both watch as she sears the tip of the metal implement and then allows it to cool before dipping it into the vial of faerie blood she'd shown us earlier.

"You mean we aren't getting your fresh blood?" I ask.

She shakes her head. "There's no need since I have

this vial."

"Then it's just the two of us who will suffer the bite of the needle, Quinn," I say to my comrade who just shrugs at me.

"Seems a small price to pay," he answers. I agree.

"Who's first?" Tink asks.

"Me," Quinn answers, hurrying over before I can protest. Of course, I have no intention of protesting, but he doesn't know that.

I'm more interested in seeing what happens when she pricks his skin before she does the same to me. It isn't that I don't trust her or that I'm afraid. I'm just more curious about what she's doing than in a hurry to have it done.

I watch with rapt attention as she slowly sinks the needle into Quinn's skin, just above his heart. She pulls it out again and then dips it into the vial of her golden blood, sucking up more, making sure she uses enough but not so much that she runs out before each of us is tattooed. When she's finished, she smiles broadly at her creation—a tattoo, roughly the size of my hand. It laces Quinn's chest in the shape of a delicate pair of golden Fae wings that flash iridescent colors when hit with the light.

"Marked by a Seelie Fae Princess," Quinn grins as he looks down at his chest, the tattoo placed purposely just to the left top of his heart.

"Do you feel anything?" I ask. "Do you feel different?"

"Mayhap. Jist a tinglin' sort o' sensation where

154

Tink tattooed me, but naethin' more."

"You will," Tinker replies, heating the needle again above the flame as she readies it for me. I sit down, taking off my shirt to expose my own chest and watch with great interest as she pricks the needle with her blood and then begins the tattoo. It feels like the sting of a mosquito bite repeatedly—nothing I can't handle. She quickly makes a few dots, interlacing them to create the upper wing, but then stops, frowning at it.

"What?" I start, suddenly feeling a burning sensation that runs along the arch she's made.

"It's not," she begins, but loses her voice as she takes a deep breath. "Right."

I look down to see that the shape she's tattooed on me is a deep red, not the golden color of Quinn's, but a heated crimson. It looks as if she's burned me with a branding iron. It rages hot against my chest, feeling like my skin has been set on fire and then settles into what looks like an antique gold color, darker in color than Quinn's, but still metallic in appearance.

"The hellhound," Tink says as she looks up at me, eyes wide. "It's still with you."

I shake my head, not understanding how that can be. "No. You sent it back to wherever it came from."

It's her turn to shake her head. "No, Peter. I *contained* it. I stopped it from doing damage by using my power against it to seal it away, but it's still in your veins, in your bloodstream, in *you*. And now…" She takes another deep breath. "I think it's reacting to my blood, interlacing itself in a way that binds it to you...

and to me." She looks at Quinn. "To *us*."

"What do we do?" I demand, starting to panic because this certainly doesn't sound good. "How do we stop it?"

"We can't," Tink says, looking from me to Quinn, who considers us both with a concerned expression. "We finish the tattoo so our bond keeps the hellhound contained, but its presence will keep our power tied up."

"Whit does that mean?" Quinn asks.

She looks at him. "It means we'll need to find another way to gain the extra power we need—another way to activate and strengthen the bond between us."

"And what way is that?" I ask.

She looks down for a moment and then back up at me, her face flushed with what looks like a mixture of embarrassment and hope.

"Sex."

"Sex?" I repeat, not understanding how such a simple act could be the answer to what seems like a complicated problem. "Of course, I'm not opposed to such things, but why?"

"We need the connection," she answers simply.

"You had sex with Quinn, but you still felt he needed the tattoo," I say as she shakes her head.

"We never… consummated things fully," she says, dropping her gaze to her fidgeting hands. "I'm afraid I'm still… a maid, where *that's* concerned."

"I see," I answer as I watch her continue with the tattoo on my chest, finishing it hurriedly as I wince

156

with pain, the hellhound making sure I feel his presence in every tiny prick of my skin.

She continues on with the small tattoo as I bite my lip to keep from crying out with the pain. When she's finished, I look down to find the heated red crimson marking the tattoo. Tink holds her hands above it and closes her eyes as her lips move and slowly the pain recedes. The gold of her blood takes over the lines of the tattoo which were previously red—a mark of the hellhound. Soon, the pain is gone and the entire tattoo is glowing a deep gold-red. The color is different to Quinn's—much more a burnt amber than gold.

"All done," she says as she opens her eyes and I breathe a sigh of relief.

There's silence as she mixes our blood with her own and prepares the needle again, deftly tattooing the same set of simple faerie wings just above and to the side of her heart. I can feel the connection from the moment she begins, a sort of electrical surge tingling along my veins beside the fire of the hellhound.

"Do ye think this will help us to save Fantasia?" Quinn asks.

"It can't hurt," she answers, cleaning off her needle before putting it away. "The three of us are now stronger than we were moments ago."

I consider that for a few seconds. If we can save Fantasia, then we can save Neverland from itself, as well. I look toward Quinn and he shrugs, walking out of the room without another word. Tink watches him go, as do I.

"Is he alright?" she asks.

I nod and then sigh. "That's a complicated question, I'm afraid."

"Should we go after him?"

I shake my head. "When Quinn walks away, it's because he needs his own space, time to himself. It's always best to let him go so he can battle his demons in private. Sometimes, that's all a man needs."

Turning back to me, she nods and then just holds my gaze as it becomes quite clear to both of us that we're alone. I can see the desire in her eyes, the link between us already binding us. She's so tiny and beautiful.

"I'm pleased to be bonded with the two of you," I say, breaking the silence. "And now I believe it's time for us to further that bond."

She nods, and there's a sense of trepidation in her smile. The trepidation doesn't last long though. Soon she begins to undress, letting her clothes fall to the floor until she stands before me, perfect in her naked form. Her wings spread out, their shimmering colors catching the light from the lanterns around us. I'm frozen, suddenly overcome with feelings of anxiety that make little sense to me. It's then that I realize I'm feeling Tink's emotions. Hardly like the confident and self-possessed man I would be with a naked sprite offering herself for the taking.

She walks slowly toward me, positioning herself toe to toe, and leans up, kissing me gently. A surge of heat warms me, flowing through me as I reach out to

158

stroke her wings. I note how they change colors as she gets excited. I then focus on the sweetness of her mouth and the velvety soft feel of her wings beneath my fingertips.

I pause, undressing as she watches eagerly. Her eyes hesitate on my cock and she reaches for it, touching it lightly. It responds by immediately growing harder and longer and she giggles, reminding me of her innocence. I pull her back to me. I'm hard and ready, longing to be inside her, but I know I must take my time. I want her to enjoy this and since it will be her first time, I know she'll experience pain. I wonder if she knows that, but I decide not to bring it up—not to make her worry. Instead, I take my time touching her, focusing on every curve and crevice of her delightful body.

Our lips meet again as my fingers caress her erect nub between her thighs and she closes her eyes, letting out a high-pitched moan. I slip a finger inside her already dripping center and she emits a gasp. I pause, afraid I've done something wrong, but she tells me to continue and I oblige, slowly milking her silky folds as she coos and moans in my arms. I'm about to burst as I bring her to orgasm, but I hold back, content to let her enjoy her climax and then give her another before I lay her back on the nearby bed and position myself above her.

"Are you ready?" I ask.

"I've been ready since well before I knew you," she responds, as I chuckle.

I ease into her slick tightness, enjoying the way her tiny orifice wraps around my aching cock. It's then that I remember her maidenhead and deciding it would be best to break it quickly, I thrust forward as she cries out and then I pause.

"Are you okay?" I ask.

She nods as I start to glide back and forth again, kissing her neck and the side of her face with small kisses—an apology for hurting her, though I know doing so is inevitable in this situation.

Our bodies glide back and forth in a perfectly timed dance as my lips trail across her lovely skin, her wings spread out beneath her, still flashing from one bright color to another as she bucks her hips toward mine, pulling me into her depths until I can no longer hold back.

She explodes with another orgasm, her entire body shaking as she clenches her eyes shut and throws her head back, a loud moan echoing from her. And it's then that I realize I can't hold back any longer. I haven't lasted very long, it's true, but I can't fight the need for release that completely overcomes me.

"I'm going to come," I groan.

"Don't stop. Fill me," she breathes.

My body shakes violently as I climax in a way I've never experienced before—a blinding late erupts behind my eyes and I can feel her heartbeat beating in time with mine. I've never felt so connected to someone before. I collapse against her for a moment and then lean up on one elbow, looking down at her with a soft smile. I'm panting.

"I've never felt anything like that before," I smile.

"It was amazing," she tells me, "and look."

I look toward my chest where the tattoo is no longer the rustic gold color the hellhound had caused with his tainted presence. It's now the same gold as hers and Quinn's, sending colors out as the nearby lantern shines across my chest.

I smile and kiss her again, moving off her and climbing onto the bed so she can lay quietly on my chest.

This feels perfect.

SIXTEEN
QUINN

I can feel the bond flowing from Peter to Tink and then back to me, a shared bond between the three of us. I don't feel the hellhound, as it seems to be locked into Peter, unable to escape the bonds of his body, thanks to Tink. I'd been afraid it might somehow taint one or all of us, but that doesn't seem to be the case.

Though it feels strange to be part of two other people this way, it's also something that feels... right somehow. Peter and I have always been close, closer even than brothers. My brother has certainly been a disappointment, to put things mildly. Peter though... we've been together through thick and thin, thus it almost makes sense that we should share the same woman.

And Tink... I care about her. I've been drawn to her from the moment I first laid eyes on her, and I'm proud to think of her as my woman... *our* woman. Although sharing Tink is no longer an issue for me, because I've had time to rightly process it and in processing it, decide there's no other man I'd be more willing to share her with than Peter, it still stings a bit to know he's buried within her as I seek my solitude.

I can't explain why I had to get away after she tattooed us both—just that I felt this surge of emotion hit me and I needed to process the feelings alone. And now? Now, I wait outside their door, giving them privacy while they make their bond. I shuffle back and forth, pacing before the door as I listen to Tink's moans and my own cock grows hard at the sounds. I want nothing more than to bury it within her, but I want to give them their own time together. I know I'll have my time with her, as well, but I find myself growing impatient.

"Quinn, are you out there?" Tink calls from beyond the closed door. Clearly, she could hear my pacing.

I give a gentle knock on the door before opening it and stepping into the room, to find Peter lying beside her on the bed and her naked beside him, both of them looking at me.

"Are you okay?" she asks.

I nod. "Ah apologize for leavin' as Ah did—it jist was… overwhelmin'—the feelings that overcame me."

"It's okay," Tink responds and then pats the space beside her. "Come lay next to me," she finishes as I approach the two of them and Peter smiles at me invitingly. I sit beside her and she takes my hand, placing it over one of her naked breasts. My cock only hardens further.

"Can you feel the link between us all?" she asks.

"Aye."

"Slip into bed beside me, Quinn," she says as she

yanks me down and kisses me on the lips. "We've not had time to genuinely enjoy one another like we should."

I don't wait. Instead, I immediately strip off my clothing and slip into the bed beside her, pulling her close to me and kissing her, letting her moans fill my mouth as I search her mouth with my tongue. Peter is behind her, but I put him out of my mind for the moment, focusing on Tink and only her as he strokes her wings, seemingly enjoying the colors as they flash in the growing darkness as the sun sets outside.

Bringing my mouth down to her breasts, I take my time suckling them. My hand slips between her thighs, eager to please her, and I find she's already soaked with wetness, ready for me. I won't have to ready her as she's already warm. Hot even. It's just as well, because I can't wait. The sudden urge to feel her from the inside is all-consuming and situating her beneath me, I pull her legs up beside my hips, holding her around the knees as I slip inside her, letting her folds caress my hardness. I push as deeply into her center as I can and remain there, just enjoying the feel of her slick tightness as she holds my cock within her. How long has it been since I felt a woman? I can't even answer the question and I fear thoughts of Mistress Chamir returning so I force the thoughts out of my mind and only pay attention to the stunning woman beneath me.

"Please, Quinn," she breathes, clearly wanting me to get on with it.

"In time," I reply, nuzzling her neck and kneading

her small but perky breasts. Whereas I was impatient to be inside her just moments before, now I want to take my time, let her juices soak my cock as I tease her. She shifts slightly, sending a shiver down my spine as I begin to slip free, easing almost fully out of her center before slipping inside again.

"Mmm," she mumbles while I continue making love to her slowly and delicately until I can't take it anymore. Our bodies move against one another, the friction driving me to the brink and shoving me over the edge in almost perfect unison with her own climax.

And knowing Peter watches me, watches *us*, is somehow… the icing on the cake. It stokes a fire within me I wasn't even aware was there. I like the fact that he watches, that he doesn't partake but appreciates the sight before him, all the same.

Her teeth sink lightly into my shoulder as her body shakes with another orgasm. I explode along with her and the tingle in my veins expands, pulsating through me with the power of the bond forged between the three of us, now somehow supercharged. I wonder if it feels as strong for them as it does for me.

Sated, Tink lays pressed against my chest, my cock still inside her as it slowly grows limp. Peter wraps himself around her from the other side so she's the center of our sandwich.

This feels… right. It feels like I've suddenly arrived home after being gone for far too long. From now on, wherever we go, our home will be with her. Together. The three of us.

We settle in to get a good night's sleep. Tomorrow will prove to be a treacherous day as we voyage on to Sweetland. Peter and I are no longer Lost Boys. We're men with a woman whom we both love and who loves us. We'll take our ship and continue across the horizon toward the adventure that awaits us.

***

TINKER

The voyage to Sweetland has been long, seeming to take far longer than it should, thanks to the tricks and spells that seem to wrinkle time as we know it. It's no doubt the spells are the work of Agatha and Septimus—tricks designed to keep unwanted visitors away.

Once we reach the river that leads toward our destination, I sigh a breath of relief. But, that relief is short-lived because we'll need every ounce of power for the fight that lies ahead of us.

"That doesnae look good," Hook exclaims as we approach the loch separating the river from the massive moat that surrounds the town.

I glance at him with a puzzled look. I was surprised he'd asked to accompany us on the trip, but he'd insisted, all the same. Zegar wanted nothing to do with Hook and chose to ride on the *Siren's Song* with Hook's crew rather than sharing a ship with the captain, himself. And that's just as well, because I can't deal with Zegar's expressions of distrust where I'm concerned. He knows I'm keeping something from him—the bonding between Peter, Quinn and I. Yet, I don't have the heart to tell him what's happened. I'm not sure why, since Zegar has never expressed any romantic interest in me… Still, I find myself trying to avoid the subject altogether.

As regards Zegar and Hook—it isn't likely that Zegar will ever forgive Hook any more than Peter will. Only Quinn seems to have made at least some level of peace with his brother.

"Ah'm nae aboot to let me wee brother go into yet another battle without me," Hook had said when he insisted on riding aboard the *Little White Bird.*

Of course, Quinn didn't appreciate Hook's affectionate term for him of 'wee' any more than he appreciated Hook insisting they ride on the same ship. And from the moment Hook had set foot on the ship, Quinn had made himself scarce. Not that Hook noticed—in general, he seems quite oblivious to the feelings of others—or perhaps he just doesn't care how Quinn feels about the fact that he clearly wants to make amends.

Hook's undying need to make good with Quinn makes me a bit fonder of Hook, and he'd already proven to be a valuable asset with his knowledge of the sea and the land around us. Even if the others can't see it, I believe him to be a changed man. Furthermore, I feel Hook truly has all of our best interests at heart.

And now, I look ahead, following Hook's gaze to what appears to be fog rising from the moat. Fog? No. Steam.

"Why is it steaming?" I ask, but he needn't answer me. As we grow closer, I can see the bubbles of the boiling water. I answer my own question, albeit with another one: "How is it boiling?"

"Ah think it has somethin' to do with them," Quinn says, sounding uneasy as he points at what appear to be dots on the horizon, but are really hellhounds sitting along the shore. Some of them are almost fully immersed in the shallow water at the edge, leaving just enough of themselves out of the water in order to keep alight with flame. Shimmering streaks of color run along the water in front of them.

"They've added some sort of oil to keep the fire spreading along the water's edge. It's so hot there, it's boiling the entire moat," Peter says from nearby.

Hook powers down the ship, signaling his first mate on *Siren's Song* to do the same. We let the ships drift for a bit while we figure out what to do. Simply dropping anchor might make us sitting ducks.

From what I can recall of Sweetland, there had never been a moat here before. Thus, I believe the moat has been created for this exact purpose—as a deterrent to keep anyone from interfering with the evil that's been foisted on the innocent people of Sweetland. Even from out here, I can see the darkness cast across the usually colorful candy fields that surround the castle grounds. It's going to be harder than I thought to get in.

"We could fly over," I say, not wanting to expend any more magic than I need to, but knowing we aren't going to get far out here on the water. With hellhounds keeping the water alight, we'll all boil alive in the time it takes to get across it and even if we somehow manage to survive, the hellhounds will finish us off once we clear the sizzling water surrounding the entire city.

"Not with those bastards sitting there, waiting on us to do just that," Peter says, pointing toward a row of trees that sits a bit further back from the bank of the moat. It's hard to see through the licorice limbs and the fruit rope branches that hang full of candy corn and candied cherries, but I can just make out the trebuchets lined up behind them, ready to knock out both the *Little White Bird* and the *Siren's Song* before we get anywhere near Sweetland.

We stand there, doing nothing but looking forlornly at the situation ahead of us for what feels like forever. Finally, Peter breaks the silence.

"I still have some of the pixie dust the Blue Faerie gave me. I could fly in and take the trebuchets out so our ships can fly over."

"By yourself?" I gasp.

"Well, I'm linked to you, so not *totally* by myself."

"There are too many of them, Peter," I insist. "There's no way you can take them out, even *with* my magic aiding you."

"Yeah, but they're only manned by a single loader. If I can get rid of enough of them so the others are out of range where the ships cross, we could make it."

"And the hounds? There are hundreds of them along the water's edge. Do you think they're going to just sit on the bank and ignore you as you take out the weapons they're guarding?"

"I was hoping they wouldn't see me."

"Don't you think the one hellhound you're already dealing with is more than enough?" I ask.

"Well, we have to do something," Peter answers with a shrug. "Otherwise, we're dead in the water— literally. Do you have something else in mind?"

"Give me a moment to think," I tell him, looking at the tangled mass of hellhounds and the extensive line of trebuchets further up the bank. Beyond that, I can make out the cotton candy bushes lining the path to the castle, some of them still intact and others melted into disturbing dark shapes.

The castle.

That's where we need to go, and it will take more than just Peter trying to take on catapulting objects and the hounds of hell. Not to mention there's probably batmen lurking somewhere nearby. Yes, we're incredibly outnumbered, even with Hook's crew fighting by our side. Not to mention, it's daytime so Prince Payne can't be relied on.

What to do… what to do… what to do…

Then it strikes me: the simplest plan is always the best plan because it provides for fewer things to go wrong.

"I have an idea," I say finally.

"An idea?" Hook repeats.

"Yes, but you're probably going to think I'm crazy," I start, hoping my quickly thought up plan might be just the thing to get us into the castle walls without harm. As far as I can see it, we have no other options, crazy as my idea might be.

And it is fairly crazy. Well, really crazy, actually.

Yet, what choice do we have? We're in a dreadful situation and this might be the only way out of it. Even if it doesn't work, it's worth the chance.

SEVENTEEN
PETER

I stand, watching her as she speaks, my heart growing larger by the moment. I can't be sure if the feeling inside me is pride, or perhaps it's my growing love for her taking hold of my emotions as I watch her lay out her plans.

Growing love for her? I ask myself, as I shake my head inwardly, amazed by the truth, even as it reveals itself.

I *am* growing to love her, there's no doubt in my mind. And the more I think about it, the more real and true it becomes. And frightening because I have never loved a woman before, now that I think about it. And yet… I do love Tink.

"Get Zegar over here," Hook shouts toward the *Siren's Song*.

Zegar has been avoiding us—all three of us—obviously not pleased with the bonding between Tink, Quinn and me. Though I'm fairly sure no one has told him what's happened between the three of us, I'm sure he can sense it, all the same. And he appears quite unhappy about the whole thing, which certainly is understandable. Zegar has been Tink's only friend for an awfully long time, and now he undoubtedly feels as if he's been replaced.

Zegar crawls over the deck in his croc form and shifts back into his more human shape, if you can term him 'human' at all. Hook rolls his eyes and hands Zegar a nearby tarp to cover his nude manhood, which is certainly alarmingly large and near impossible to pry one's eyes away from.

"What's going on?" Zegar growls. "Why have we stopped advancing?"

"We can't cross the moat, because it's boiling and we can't fly over it, because there are trebuchets waiting to lob flaming balls into the side of the vessels," I explain.

"Great. I guess we'll have to go back and live with the sirens then," he replies with a shrug, as though he couldn't care less.

"Ah'm sure ye'd like that, but Tink has another idea," Hook tells him.

"And? What is it?" he asks, turning toward her and waiting for a reply, but she just smiles at him, before turning to face me.

"Tink and I are going to fly Quinn and Hook over the line of the hellhounds."

"And the rest of us are just supposed to sit here and wait for the four of you to do battle by yourselves?" Zegar demands, his tone more acidic than usual. Yes, he is certainly perturbed by the state of affairs between the three of us. I will have to have a talk with him to smooth things out later.

"Not exactly. We need a distraction."

"A distraction for what?" he demands.

"We need you to shift and… entertain the hellhounds so we can get into the city," Tink blurts out.

Zegar snaps his head toward her as if she's slapped him and then looks at the moat and all of the hellhounds lined up there.

"Ignoring the fact that you used the word '*entertain*', you want me to shift back into my croc form and take those fuckers on some sort of rabbit chase, me being the damned rabbit?"

"Yes," I answer, as Tink nods.

"And what will the four of you be doing once you get into the castle proper?" Zegar demands.

"We need to see the castle physician," Tink explains. "And then we'll demand that he make a cure for the disease that created the hellhounds and the batmen."

"And if you cure this infection of theirs?" Zegar starts. "What then?"

"Then they will return to the humans they once were," Tink answers.

"How do you intend to get this cure to the hundreds of hellhounds and batmen? Not to mention, I doubt Agatha and Septimus will just stand aside to allow you to do your business."

Tink nods and then cocks her head to the side, as she ponders his comment. "Well, we can get the cure to the hellhounds and batmen by mixing it with faerie dust and flying across them, thus sprinkling it onto them."

174

She takes a big breath. "As to Agatha and Septimus... I suppose it will come down to battle, if it must."

Zegar shakes his head. "This is much too dangerous. I've been trying to protect you all this time, Princess, not lead you to the enemy on a silver platter."

"I won't let anything happen to her, Zegar," I say.

"Aye, nor will Ah," Quinn adds.

"An' ye can count me in as well," Hook says.

Zegar regards each of us with disinterest and Hook with irritation. "That sounds both dangerous and not likely to work," Zegar groans, and taking a deep breath, seems completely unimpressed with Tink's plan.

"It will work," she insists.

"How do you know?" he nearly spits the words at her.

"Because it has to."

"Oh. Well, then. We're all set," Zegar scoffs and turns away from her, shaking his head, as though he can no longer stomach looking at her.

"Whether it works or not, it's our best plan," Tink insists. "It's only a matter of time before the hellhounds realize we're just sitting idle out here and they go on the offensive."

"Well, I always wanted to bathe in an excessively hot spring. I guess now is my opportunity," he replies.

"Let's get going, then," Tink says, clapping her hands together as she turns to face me, choosing to disregard Zegar's foul temper. "Peter, you take Quinn and I'll carry Hook."

"Lucky me," Hook says with a smile.

I glare at him, wishing him as much harm as I can summon in a single thought. I wish I was the one to carry him—then I could accidentally drop him into the line of hellhounds and be done with him, once and for all. No doubt Tink guesses as much, which is why she volunteered to carry Hook, herself. She has too soft a heart, for it seems she harbors a soft spot for the bastard. And Quinn might be in the process of forgiving Hook for what he's done, but I have no intention of doing so. I only stomach the bastard because we need him right now.

Tink touches my hand softly and looks up at me, melting me with her smile. It's hard to think about murdering a man when someone so perfect is in your sights. I turn my attention to Zegar as he assumes a perch on the front of the boat and then dives into the water ahead. A moment later, he emerges, not in his usual crocodile form, but in one that's easily ten times larger. For a moment, we all stand, watching him in stunned silence as he twists in the air and dives back into the water, swimming up the river and slipping beneath the loch.

"Showboat," Hook mutters.

A moment later, Zegar emerges again on the other side of the river, soaring high into the air like a whale out for a Sunday swim, and sends the hellhounds into a frenzy of activity. It's our cue to begin our flight, as he taunts them in his giant crocodile form.

"Let's go while they're busy with him," I say, pulling the pixie dust from my pocket and grabbing up

Quinn in my arms as I use the pixie dust to take flight.

Tink grips Hook, his larger frame dangling haphazardly in her arms, as she soars upward beside us. Luckily, her pixie dust allows her to carry anything, no matter the weight. And Hook is a weighty bastard.

It's only another few seconds before we're quickly across the loch, looking down at Zegar as he dives beneath the water and emerges in various places down the line of hellhounds, picking off as many as he can before disappearing again beneath the waves. They can't go after him for fear of extinguishing their fire completely, leaving them powerless against him.

"Incoming," Quinn calls as we appear above the moat.

Tink and I move quickly, dodging the fireballs and sharp projectiles being launched at us from the trebuchets. It's much easier to avoid them with our small forms. The ships would have never been able to do so, given the difference in mass alone. Sometimes it's certainly better to be small and thus, nimble.

Once we fly past the weapons, I shoot a glance back toward Zegar. It's beyond bizarre to see a nearly hundred foot crocodile popping up out of the water and rolling across an entire line of hellhounds, then slipping back into the water before they can touch him.

I turn back to look at our path ahead; Tink and I make haste to fly across the wafer walls surrounding Sweetland. Once inside the city, we land on a street near the castle and drop our cargo. Even though Tink and I are exhausted from our flight over, there's no time to pause or catch our breath. Instead, the four of us begin running toward the castle gates, eager to get inside so we can find this physician Tink mentioned as soon as possible.

Instead, we find ourselves grinding to a halt right outside the gates. In front of us stands a man I have never met, but the woman beside him is someone I know all too well.

"Agatha," I hiss at her.

She smiles, but she isn't looking at me. Her gaze is focused squarely on Tink. I glance in her direction to see a look of pure horror on Tink's face, but she isn't looking at Agatha. She's looking at the man standing beside Agatha. She gasps loudly and the color drains from her face. He must be the Unseelie King, Septimus.

***

TINKER

I'm frozen. I can't move. I can't speak.

I've been dreading this day for years— experiencing nightmares about it but somehow, I never thought it would come. Now that it's here, I'm useless. I don't even know how I'm still able to breathe.

Septimus killed most of my court, leaving only myself and my Aunt Saxe as survivors. I've dreamed of killing him so many times, but now I can't bring myself to as much as curse his name. Instead, I'm terrified, like a little girl who shrinks in the face of danger. Then I have to wonder if it's just my fear that holds me immobile or some sort of power he wields over me?

I decide it's the latter. His power dwarfs mine. The scales are tipped far in his favor. How could I ever have thought I could take someone like Septimus down? For all of the bravado I'd felt on the deck of the *Little White Bird*, dreaming up this plan to get the cure that could possibly end this nightmare by wiping out Septimus and Agatha's army of hellhounds and batmen, I hadn't considered that I might, instead, find myself face to face with Septimus so soon.

"Tink?" Peter almost whispers, and his voice spurs me into action, at last.

Because I have something Septimus doesn't: I have the power of my two men flowing through me and their power merged with mine means I'm much stronger than I was before.

"Niece," Septimus starts, and just the sound of his voice is enough to unleash the flood of anger and hatred within me. I summon the strength of my shared bond with Quinn and Peter to bolster my own strength as I streak toward him, acting not unlike a human cannonball. Septimus is unprepared for my attack and when I hit him, the blow knocks him backwards and off his feet, but not for long. He's quickly back up again, facing off against me as he summons a large blue fireball in his hands and thrusts it at me.

I shift to one side, avoiding the flaming ball, and it flies past me, burning a hole through the peanut brittle wall behind me. Immediately, a skeletal looking cat launches itself through the hole in the peanut brittle and shoots toward me. I fly up as the hellcat screeches past me and dissipates into thin air. Septimus comes after me then, bolting upright to match me in the air.

"You are no match for me, child," Septimus yells at me, but I don't respond. I can't—I need all my energy, all my focus.

I can't imagine what we must look like to those watching from below, each of us summoning whatever pops into our minds to lob at the other. I duck as a blue fireball goes screeching past me. I, meanwhile, channel my magic to fling the fireball off course, lest it collide with one of our ships in the distance. The fireball heads toward the river just past our ships, and fizzles once it hits the water. I immediately duck to one side as I turn back, almost getting hit with an avalanche of ice that appears from nowhere.

I summon Chinese stars and hurl them at him, hoping at least some of them will do enough damage to reduce his focus, but he easily parts them in the middle, sending them flying past him on either side.

"Is that the best you can do, niece? Surely the Blue Faerie taught you better magic than that," he says.

I hurl a lump of bubble gum at him, sealing his mouth shut before he can taunt me further. Yes, it's ridiculous, but the image pops into my head and before I can think of another action, I've already created it.

Septimus' mention of the Blue Faerie has affected my focus, just as he intended, but I'm not about to let him end me quite so easily. While he snatches the gum from his mouth, I unleash a murder of crows to scratch

180

and claw at him.

They alight on him, doing their best to peck his eyes out, but he quickly banishes them into the ethers with a sinister laugh as he reaches upward and forms a large mace above his head. The spiked ball is much larger than such a weapon is usually and he swings it around by its handle, letting go of the entire thing so it hurls speedily toward my head.

I close my wings, letting myself fall abruptly so the ball sails over my head. Then I resume flight as I conjure up my own magic to counter him. Summoning as much power as I can muster from myself, Peter, and Quinn, I point a finger in his direction, sending several bolts of lightning toward him and missing with the first two. The third catches him, but just barely, leaving a gash across his upper arm that's little more than a flesh wound.

I fly across the Sweetland sky, with Septimus in pursuit, eager to pull the fight away from Peter and Quinn. I can use their power, but I want to make sure their physical forms remain safe. They can handle Agatha on their own.

A flock of black vultures appears out of the midst around Septimus and charges me. I weave and bob, avoiding most of them, but one hits me mid-center, sending me flying backwards, causing me to lose altitude and land on top of a candy-cane trellis, leading to the castle. Candy cane pillars snap loudly as I crash against them.

"Do you really think you're any match for my

power?" Septimus taunts me, landing on the ground in front of me.

I shriek as he reaches out and grabs me by the arm, flinging me sideways and sending me sailing across the yard, toward a small gingerbread hut. I hit the wall full force, crumbling it as I slide into the front room, which is empty. All of Sweetland is empty, owing to the fact that Agatha and Septimus have turned all its residents into their own army of horrors.

I shoot back into the air, flying quickly toward the field of gum drops situated beside the frosted sugar glass castle atrium. I turn to find Septimus closing in on me, taunting me in a voice that sounds like it's coming more from inside my head than from his mouth. It rattles around inside me, confusing me as it echoes around my mind.

Do you think you can kill me like you did your aunt? His voice assaults my mind.

He knows!

That's right, he laughs acidly. *Of course, I know the truth, Tinker. We're not so different, you and I. Are we?*

"You and I are nothing alike!" I shout at him because I don't want to mind-speak with him—it just seems too intimate, too close.

Although you might despise the truth, you know it, all the same, he says, his voice now sounding like it's in triplicate as it bounces around in my head.

"You're a monster! I'm nothing like you," I hiss at him.

182

Are you so certain?

He sounds closer, impossibly close, but I can't see him. He's not in front of me anymore, but I can hear him all around me. I jerk my head from side to side and then whirl around, realizing I can feel him behind me. I dart to one side, headed back over the castle walls, but I'm too late.

The ripping sound fills the air around us, echoing against the candy walls of the castle. At the same time, pain shoots through my body, and I find myself falling, spiraling toward the ground. Septimus floats above me, laughing as he holds one of my wings upward as if to signal victory.

I don't feel the pain of hitting the ground.

Everything has already gone black.

EIGHTEEN
QUINN
Twenty minutes earlier

I want to go after Tink, to protect her against Septimus, but I can't. Instead, I'm stuck here to deal with Agatha and the batmen she's summoned to fight her battles for her. Behind me, I can hear the nightmarish howls of the hellhounds as they come inland, giving up their fight with Zegar to heed the call of their masters.

Hook and I pull our swords, fighting off the batmen back to back. We can't hold them off much longer, not with those rabid dogs soon to join them within minutes. Something has to give or we're goners.

"Hook, this seems like a suitable time to tell ye Ah forgive ye."

"Tell me after the fight is over."

"Ah'm afraid we might nae be speakin' when this fight is over, at least nae in any language either o' us would understand."

"Good point," Hook answers.

I nod. "Nae matter whit happens, we're square. That's all."

"Thanks, now get yer head back in this fight so we

184

can have a pint later to celebrate our brotherly reunion."

I spear one of the batmen, as it shrieks toward me and cast it aside, preparing for another, but instead, I find myself facing Agatha who stands at a healthy distance with a sickening smile across her face.

"You're outmatched, Quinn. You won't be so lucky as you were last time."

"Lucky?" I scoff, thinking of the last time I crossed paths with her—the time she cursed us.

She chuckles and the sound grates on me. If I thought I hated my own brother, that feeling was nothing compared to the anger and disgust I harbor for this woman.

"You think a little curse of immortality is bad?" she continues to laugh. "It's nothing compared to what I'll do to you this time. I was far too merciful before. I won't be again."

"My, my, arenae ye the petty, bitter one?" Hook says, turning so he's facing Agatha while I continue to fight off yet another of the batmen from the other side.

"I've nothing to be bitter about," she says, sounding far more wounded than certain of that fact.

"Och, come now, Aggie," Hook calls her by the name he used to—when they were lovers all those years ago—before Agatha ever became the coldblooded, venomous bitch she now is.

"We both know ye were in love with me," Hook continues and I wonder what the bloody hell he's doing. Enraging the bitch isn't the way to handle this situation.

185

"What are you talking about?" she demands, her cheeks coloring in such a way that it's quite obvious Hook speaks the truth.

"Ye couldnae handle me nae feelin' the same towards ye," he continues. "Ye're naethin' more than a jilted, shame-faced and rejected woman actin' oot her vengeance."

"That's not true," she shrieks at him.

Even without seeing her, I can hear the truth in her voice—everything he said is honest. And, what's more, he's getting under her skin. I can also see it in the actions of the batman I'm battling. With Agatha's attention focused elsewhere, the creature seems a bit more hesitant, slow to react. It's as if he's confused by what he's doing, but still feels compelled to do it.

"Ye can deny it all ye want, but we both know 'tis absolutely the truth. Ye cursed me an' the Lost Boys because ye cared far more for all o' us than any o' us did for ye. An' ye couldnae handle that, could ye?"

"I…" she starts but her words falter as Hook continues.

"Because ye were overcome with anger an' hatred, ye wanted yer revenge so ye made sure we were stuck in time, doomed to all eternity. That was yer plan, but it didnae work, did it? Even with yer curse, we managed to prevail. An' that means ye failed, Agatha."

"I didn't fail. I *never* fail."

"Aye, ye failed alright," he insists, nodding as he continues to glare at her. "We escaped ye an' yer power. We got away from Neverland an' we escaped ye."

"You haven't escaped me and you never will," she insists. "Each of you carries me with you in the form of the curse I placed on you. And you will never be free of that."

"For as miserable as ye are an' the curse ye put oan us all, ye didnae win. We each found love an' whit have ye got to say fer yerself? Ye have nae one, Agatha—nae one who gives a lick whether or nae ye wake oop in the mornin'. "

"Found love?" she repeats, eyeing him narrowly. Though it's clear she's attempting to school her expression, the shock is still there, all the same.

"Aye."

"With whom?"

"A princess o' the sea," Hook answers. "A good, kind an' lovely woman who owns me whole heart. A woman in every way ye arenae."

Agatha doesn't outwardly respond. She says nothing and her expression is just as poker-faced as it had been. Yet, the air around her is different—it trembles with rage and the energy fans out past her, smacking into me and making me feel as I've been struck by a ship.

I'm shocked as the batmen attacking us suddenly drop back and wait, as if stuck behind some sort of invisible shield. The howls of the hellhounds die and the sound of their hooves in the distance stop. And it's all due to Agatha—she's so angered, so devastated, so upset by Hook's rebuke, she's losing control over the creatures she's created to fight for her.

I seize the opportunity to take out the one I face, ending him with a swift stroke that separates his hideous head from his shoulders and sends the body rolling sideways. Yes, it's a shame they were once people and perhaps we can turn the survivors back into their former selves, but at this point, I still consider them enemies. It's me or them.

The others continue to linger back, frozen on their way toward me as Agatha continues to lose her control over them, instead focusing her power inward where it's being consumed by her hurt and anger.

"Break!" Hook yells suddenly, rushing forward, away from me. I turn quickly to defend my now empty back and see him launching himself against Agatha who is furiously coming at him herself, now having completely lost control of the creatures around us, as well as herself. I watch as the batmen all collapse to the ground, not dead, but neutralized by their own confusion.

The sound of something approaching resumes, but it's not the paws of the hellhounds bounding inward to attack. Instead, it's something big, stomping towards us with a heavy, rapid pace. I brace myself for whatever Agatha has summoned to attack us next, even as Hook and I attempt to subdue her with our swords. Perhaps she didn't lose as much focus as we thought, shifting it toward whatever is headed our way...

"I'm going to end you this time," she says to Hook. "I'm going to make sure you never come back and then

I'm going to do the same to all of your Lost Boys and the crews of those ships you think I don't see out in the river." She takes a breath. "And then I'm going to hunt down this princess of yours and I'm going to destroy her too—but slowly. I'll make her feel every fragment of pain I have felt since you used me and then left me to rot."

Hook reacts by lunging forward again, his sword prepared to impale her, but she sidesteps him, dodging his extended blade, only to find herself run through by mine. She never saw me as I approached, so caught up in her own rage and humiliation. Even as she's stuck by my blade, she twists around to look at me and there's shock in her gaze.

Her shrieks fill the air as Hook once again thrusts his sword forward and catches her squarely in the chest where her heart would be if she, in fact, had one. But Agatha's heart has long since shriveled up and died. We both pull our blades free in preparation to strike again if we must, but whatever she summoned is growing closer, no doubt fueled by the power remaining in her wounded form. I step back, waiting for the incoming beast to arrive as Agatha falls to the ground, blood pouring from the wounds in her abdomen and chest.

Even as she suffers, she attempts to fight back, summoning a ball of icy blue fire to lob at whichever of us she can hit, but as she pulls back her arm to send it towards us, I see our latest visitor arriving with a thunderous cacophony as he launches himself forward and opens his jaws. Both Hook and I watch with wide eyes as Zegar snaps teeth larger than us together, biting Agatha into two pieces and slinging her separate halves in either direction.

"Zegar! Good timin', me friend," Hook groans, trying to catch his breath, even as a chuckle and an enormous smile overtake his face.

Behind me, the batmen scramble to their feet and begin to flee. Toward the moat, the sound of the hellhounds running fills the air once again, this time in every direction but toward us. Hook and I breathe a sigh of relief as the confused creatures begin to scatter to the winds, now without a master to control them. We enjoy the moment, knowing there's still a battle to fight wherever Tink and Peter have gone.

A swish of air catches us off guard. I look up, just in time to see something falling fast from the sky. I blink as it hits the ground in front of us.

"Tink!" I scream, rushing toward her as she lay on the grass by Zegar's tail. He shifts back to his human form and joins me beside her, eager to lend whatever aid we can.

"Tinker," he whispers over her broken body.

I can only stare at the area of her back, which is dripping gold blood. She's missing a wing... When I realize Zegar can't bring himself to do it, I slowly turn her over to check for a pulse.

***

PETER

190

Five Minutes Earlier

I'm too late.

I see Septimus behind her, but I can't get to him fast enough. Horrified, I watch as he snatches one of her gossamer wings off her back and holds it up in victory as she begins to fall to the ground, spiraling through the air. Immediately, my concern and horror turn to fury.

I summon all the power I can from our link to soften her blow as she lands, knowing I can't catch her before she hits the ground. Instead, I use what magic I can to keep her from further harm. It's then that I feel the hellhound within me. With my own anger, it must have come to the fore because I can feel it burning deep inside me, rising to the surface, wanting to be released.

I reach out and take control of the hellhound, imagining myself wrangling it, forcing it to be obedient to me. Yes, I'll let it out, but it must obey me. I'm surprised when it allows me to slip the figurative noose of my own power over its neck. It's then that I realize—Agatha must be dead because the creature is now mine to control. And control it I will because I need its strength now more than ever before.

I use what's left of the pixie dust to sail higher into the air and then I hover in front of Septimus, ready to die if I have to in order to take this bastard out for what he's done to Tink.

"Ah, Peter Pan," he says the words with a smile of disdain on his mouth—as if it's cute or sweet that I'm going up against him. The bastard.

"Do you think you can defeat me when your little Fae beauty could not?"

"I'm willing to give it a try."

His smile falters, replaced with an ugly frown. "You are no match for me, boy. You're nothing but an irritant—a gnat," he says, waving a hand to one side as if to swat me away.

Instead, I remain firm, the power from my bond with Tink and Quinn holding steady with the hellhound's fury rising to the surface. I can feel the tattoo on my chest beginning to burn as the creature's power filters into the forefront of my mind. I'm still surprised to find it obeying my commands, but pleased all the same.

Septimus glares at me, drops Tink's wing, coming for me now, instead. I let him get close enough that he thinks he can hurt me, and then I unleash the hellhound on him. I thrust my hands forward and I can feel a burning sensation in my eyes as I narrow them at him. It's then that a hose of fire shoots out from my palms, nearly roasting him alive. His wings scorch and immediately catch fire, sending him falling to the ground, looking like a blazing comet. He hits down hard, slamming into the unforgiving earth and then rolling near Tink on the other side of Zegar's tail.

Zegar swats him away angrily, sending his charred and broken body crashing against a nearby ice cream cone house. The house topples and falls on Septimus, pinning him beneath its rainbow sprinkled top. If Tink weren't hurt, I'd laugh, but my mind is on her now and there's nothing humorous about her lying on the grass nearby.

She isn't moving.

Quinn kneels beside her as I hurry over and lean over him. Zegar kneels right beside Quinn, and no one says a word.

"Is she…" I start but can't finish.

"She has a pulse," Quinn answers.

"I can feel her life force within the bond," I answer with a quick nod, feeling that little shining ball of energy that is Tink.

Quinn looks up at me. "Do ye think we could heal her with the bond?"

I shrug. I don't know how the bond works, but I figure it's worth a shot. I just nod and thinking it might help, I take his hand. Then I place my free hand on Tink, and Quinn does the same.

"Whit should we do?" Quinn asks.

I shrug, because his guess is as good as mine. "I think… just close your eyes and funnel whatever energy you have into her. Imagine her healing."

He nods and I do as I told him. I imagine everything within me flowing through my arm and down into my hand, the energy leaving my fingers and entering Tink's prone form. I imagine a bright, white light settling over her entire body, feeding her the healing energy she needs.

When I open my eyes, I find Quinn's still shut tight. A few seconds later, he opens them and looks at me. Then we both look at Tink. Her chest continues to rise and fall with her subdued breathing, but she doesn't stir, doesn't open her eyes.

"Ah dinnae think it worked," Quinn whispers.

"She moved," Zegar points out.

"Aye, ye should close yer eyes an' do it agin," Hook says, from where he stands above us.

I nod to Quinn, and we do the same thing again. This time, I crunch my eyes shut tightly, as tightly as I can and I imagine all of my energy pouring out of me, joining with Quinn's and sinking into Tink, healing her, bringing her back from the precipice.

I open my eyes, to find Quinn's already open. It's another few seconds before Tink comes to, blinking a few times as she looks at both of us and appears confused. She closes her eyes and then opens them again, before a wobbly smile takes hold of her lips.

"Guess I'm still alive," she manages in a battle worn voice.

Each of us smiles in turn, but no one makes any motion to gather her into his arms—we're all still too concerned about the state of her fragile, little body.

"Ye had us, lass," Quinn admits, breathing out a sigh of relief. "We thought we'd nearly lost ye, there."

"Can you move?" I ask.

She lifts her arms up and then wiggles her fingers. Then she looks at me. "I think so."

She attempts to sit up and Zegar reaches a hand forward, on her lower back, helping to push her upright. Then she just sits there for a few seconds, before looking at me. "I feel okay."

I nod and watch as she attempts to stand, Zegar and Quinn hovering beside her like overly concerned nursemaids. She's shaky and off balance, but she's suddenly alert, looking around for Septimus.

"Where is he?" she asks.

"I unleashed the hellhound within me and set him on fire. He crashed into a house over there," I answer and point towards the direction I last saw Septimus. Tink immediately starts walking, or rather *limping*, in that direction before Zegar puts a giant hand on her shoulder to stop her.

"Tink, you need to take things slowly," I tell her. "That was quite the fall you took."

She looks at me and frowns. "Don't treat me like a helpless firefly," she replies, pushing me aside as she frees herself from Zegar and then stumbles toward Septimus, who has begun to move. Dammit, I'd thought him for sure dead.

I can feel her pulling at me with her magic as she gathers what strength she can from myself and Quinn and directs it toward Septimus, raising her arms up in front of her. Then I watch as Septimus' body begins to rise from the mess of the ice cream cone house, sending splinters of the cone through the air as she lifts him with our combined magic. Tink flings her hand to one side and Septimus goes sailing through the air, not just across the marshmallow field in front of the castle walls, but across the moat and beyond, his body growing smaller and smaller the further away he soars, until finally, he blips out of sight.

She lowers her hand then and her shoulders hunch forward, her strength clearly drained, but she waves off Zegar as he tries to help her.

"Where did you send him?" I ask.

"Away. Far outside the city to give us some time to heal and to reverse the curse of the hellhounds and the batmen."

"Then he's not dead?"

She shakes her head. "He's strong. He'll recover and come back."

"Then you should have let us finish him," I announce, jaw tight.

Tink looks at me and shakes her head again. "You can't finish him, Peter. His magic is too strong, even with him injured."

"We can if we all work together," I insist.

"We don't have enough power left," she answers, looking over her shoulder at her missing wing. She doesn't react, other than to take a deep breath and then face me again. "We're too weak now, Peter. We need time to heal, to reassess the situation. But, with Agatha dead and Septimus' army wiped out, we've dealt him a good blow."

I nod, because I see her point. "Then we will rest and heal. And once we're returned to full health, we'll make a plan to come after him and get rid of him for good."

Tink agrees with a quick nod. Then she takes a deep breath and looks from Quinn to me. "We have to get to the physician and cure these people of their plague."

"Tink, you're still hurt," I point out.

"Aye, ye're bleedin'," Quinn tells her.

"I'm fine," she insists, still wavering on her feet. I pull my shirt off and put it over her, letting the material soak up the blood from her missing wing as we head toward the doors of the castle. I'm overcome with worry for her—I'm not sure what she'll do with a missing wing. How will she ever fly again?

She must be able to sense my sadness, because she turns to me with a reassuring smile and pats my hand. "It's okay, Peter. There's more than one way to fly."

I smile back at her. "You're right. And you'll never fall again, as long as I'm by your side."

NINETEEN
TINKER

"Thank you, Doctor," I tell the castle physician as he finishes bandaging up the wound where Septimus tore off my wing and then turns to face a large wood armoire. He opens one of the doors and reaches for a large glass bottle, turning to face me again.

"I had the antidote already mixed," he explains, before sighing. "I never wanted to do the things Agatha and Septimus forced me to do to the townspeople of Sweetland. It was my hope that someone would defeat them, thus I had the elixir ready to go."

I accept the bottle of glowing green liquid and thank him again. I had a feeling he'd been forced into doing Agatha and Septimus' bidding, so I'm not surprised to find such is the case.

"Do you require assistance?" The nice old man asks.

"Just in rounding up all the batmen and hellhounds," I answer. Now that I'm missing my wing, I can't create any more fairy dust (and Peter's out of the ration the Blue Faerie gave him) and I can't fly above the hellhounds and batmen, trying to sprinkle the cure on top of them. So that means we're going to have to round them up the old fashioned way.

I'm hopeful that with the added power I have from Quinn and Peter, I'll be able to grow another wing. It's a tall order and I won't even attempt it until I'm fully healed and rested, but my hope is that between the three of us, we'll be able to manage it.

We take the glass bottle to the lab next to his exam room and begin our work, filling as many small syringes with the cure as we can find. Apparently, it will just take a few drops of the antidote to cure each creature.

Rounding up all the creatures is exhausting work. Even though Agatha is no longer dictating their actions, they're still feral and we have to be careful. After a few hours, we have them gathered within the walls of the castle courtyard (led there with hunks of beef as a lure) and we begin inoculating each and every one of them as they feed. It's a simple process of sticking them with the syringes—something the hellhounds barely feel through their thick fur. The batmen are a bit trickier, but we accomplish their inoculations by shooting them with darts laced with the antidote.

"Tink, ye need to rest," Quinn tells me again.

"I'm so sick and tired of every one saying that."

"Well, we mean it. Ye need to heal yerself, dinnae forget."

"Not until every last citizen of Sweetland is cured," I answer, taking a big breath because we're almost finished with exactly that. "Where's Peter?"

"He jist returned from the forest."

"The forest?"

Quinn nods. "Aye, he an' Zegar have been roundin' up the hellhounds that wouldnae enter the castle courtyard an' treatin' them."

"Oh, good," I answer, pleased with how everything is coming together.

"Ah believe they should be finished with the final hellhound shortly," Quinn continues.

I nod. "When they are, will you send Peter to see me? He needs to be treated too and I think he's been avoiding me."

"Aye."

"Thanks."

I lean toward him and kiss him on the cheek. I feel the familiar ache I always feel towards him, but there's no time to sate either of our needs. I need to find Peter and give him a shot of the cure so the hellhound inside him is put to rest, once and for all. At that point, we'll be free to leave Sweetland and we can start our journey to Bloodstone Castle, where I'll get to see Aunt Saxe again, after all these years.

It's another few minutes before I hear the sounds of Quinn's and Peter's voices as they echo down the castle hall.

"Are you ready?" I ask him when the door opens to our bedroom and Peter walks inside.

"Yes," he tells me when I approach him. "But, there's a question about this that's been nagging at me."

"What do you mean?" I ask.

"Well, I got infected by a spark from one of the hellhound's fires—I didn't become a hellhound, myself. So what happens if you give me the cure? It's not as though the hellhound within me can become a person again because there's no person attached to it."

I nod. "I'd considered the same thing and I'm not sure what the answer is."

"Then… maybe we should just skip this whole thing?"

I frown at him. "You can't just let that thing stay inside you."

"Why not?" he answers, his chin held high as I wonder what in the world he's thinking. "The power of the beast is held in check by the tattoo you gave me."

"So what?"

"So that means I can control the hellhound."

"But, why would you want to?" I ask, shaking my head as I frown at him.

"Because it gives me extra power. It was the only reason I was able to take down Septimus, and I might need to use the power of the hellhound again. Who knows what we still might face?"

He has a point, but I'm not sure it's such a good idea. "Peter, we don't know what the hellhound is capable of."

"With Agatha gone, I'm not worried about it. I can control it and I want to hold on to it, at least until after our battles are behind us."

"You're sure?" I repeat.

He nods. "Just save me a vial of the cure—in case I ever need it."

"Suit yourself," I answer with a shrug. "I'm not

entirely sure it's a good idea, but I'll do as you ask."
And knowing the hellhound within him was never
actually a person before... then I guess no harm, no
foul.

"Thank you," he replies, pulling me into his
embrace. The ache I felt earlier is strong now, but I'm
so weary... bone tired, really.

When we finally finish giving out the vaccines, I
start to fully feel the full weight of the days we've put
behind us—days filled with fear and angst. The worst
of it finally appears to be past us... at least, for now. Of
course, Septimus will be back, but I'm hoping by then,
I'll be ready for him.

We'll be ready for him.

"I'm going to go get some sleep for a while," I tell
him, and he nods.

"Do you want me to join you?"

"Yes," I answer with a big smile. There's nothing
I'd like more. "Bring Quinn with you. I sleep better
when I'm curled up with both of you."

***

More than a week later, the four of us finally set
off for Maura LeChance's castle, Bloodstone. It's the
same place where Prince Payne had been held prisoner
for all those years. He seems only too eager to return to
Briar Rose, though. And as we are leaving in the
evening, he's along for the ride, rather than buried in
the ship's sleeping quarters.

Because I can't power the ship with my fairy dust,

owing to my missing wing, we're sailing to Bloodstone
Castle the old fashioned way.

When we leave Sweetland, the townspeople are
incredibly grateful to us. Even though they don't
understand what happened to them or what they'd been
turned into, they're left with horrible memories they
scarce understand. Sweetland truly is a town in
recovery. The once beautiful, candied landscape is now
faded from neglect. A large section of the marshmallow
fields had been scorched by hellhounds, and the bats
had torn apart many of the homes in the area.

But, the residents seem excited and anxious to
restore Sweetland to its former glory, already tearing
down broken and crumbling gingerbread houses and
replacing broken candy cane street lights and the
caramel roads. A part of me would love to stay and help
them, but I still have work to do and I can't just hide
away in Sweetland forever…

So, now we find ourselves back on board the *Little
White Bird*, heading for our next adventure. Because
it's a long voyage, over the neverending miles of water,
I'm pleased to find I can rest instead of having to use
my powers to keep the ship afloat.

It's a relief when we finally dock a few days later
and step onto dry land. It feels odd not being able to fly,
owing to my missing wing, but I suppose I'll get used
to it. I hope so, anyway.

I retire to my makeshift room—situated in the
upstairs portion of an old inn in some harbor town in
which we've stopped for the night. Now that I'm well-

rested and healed from my injuries, I feel my need for Peter and Quinn growing stronger. I strip down naked and stand before them in our room, feeling oddly self-conscious with only one wing.

"Whit's wrong, Tink?" Quinn asks as he approaches me, cupping my chin in his hands, and pulling my face up towards his.

"I just feel… like less than I used to be," I say softly, unable to meet his sweet gaze.

"Why would ye say such a thing? Ye're the same Tink ye always were."

"I only have one wing, and there's an ugly scar where the other one used to be," I answer, feeling the sting of tears in my eyes. I was hoping time would help ease the pain of losing part of me, but it hasn't really at all. And the more I want to try to heal myself, the more nervous I get because… what if I can't do it? What if *we* can't do it and I'm stuck this way forever? No more flying, no more pixie dust, no more… magic.

If such is the case, I'll never have a shot in hell of going up against Septimus.

"Well, you're just as beautiful as the first time I laid eyes on you," Peter says.

"You're just saying that because you love me," I respond before realizing what I'm saying. We've never discussed love, nor ever said the words to each other. And now that the words are out of my mouth, my heart starts racing because I'm suddenly afraid they aren't true. Yes, the three of us are bonded, but that doesn't mean they have to be in love with me. As to me… I am in love with them and feel as if I always have been.

"It's true," Peter says as he faces me. "I do love you and I love you however you are—with two wings or one."

"Aye, an' Ah love ye too, Tink," Quinn adds.

My heart is suddenly so full, I can't keep my tears back and they come eagerly to the surface, dripping down my cheeks.

"Ah, dinnae cry, lass!" Quinn says as he wipes them away.

"I just…" I start, as the words get swallowed by the frog in my throat. I force them out a few seconds later. "I'm just… so happy. And I… I love both of you too."

Peter smiles down at me before moving around me to kiss my shoulder blade where my wing used to be.

The two of them soothe me, Peter kissing my neck and shoulders while Quinn kisses my mouth, our tongues dancing a lazy tango as I begin to forget how self-conscious I feel. Really, it's impossible to feel self-conscious around my men—they just… they adore me and in their presence, I feel like the most beautiful woman in the world.

I begin to undress Quinn, enjoying the way his hard body presses against mine. Behind me, Peter strips away his own clothing. I turn around and kiss him as Quinn reaches between my legs and begins to massage my sensitive nub with his fingers, getting me ready for them. My legs tremble as I give in to the sensations taking over my body and allow him to bring me to climax while Peter continues to kiss me deeply.

We move toward the bed, slowly making our way in a tangle of arms, legs, and libidos. Peter curls around me while Quinn and I make love so slowly, I think I might cry against him. It feels like we're floating as our power combines, sending our bodies levitating slightly above the bed as we join one another.

Peter waits, content to just hold me as Quinn and I satisfy our hunger for one another. Finally, Peter takes me from behind, slipping into my center with one fluid stroke and cupping my breasts in his hands as he satisfies me with his considerable girth. I coo and moan as he brings me to yet another orgasm and fills me with a warm stream of his own climax.

I lean against Quinn, feeling like the luckiest woman in the world.

TWENTY
TINKER
Bloodstone Castle

Training is of the utmost importance now that we've had a chance to rest and recover. And depleting Septimus' army is certainly a start, but it's not the answer because I know how powerful he is—and that means he'll be back en force, as soon as he can regroup and come up with another plan.

In the meantime, the link between Peter, Quinn and me has created a shared source of power we're still learning how to use. Each of us has our own magic, but combined, we're a source to be reckoned with or we will be once we learn how to control and focus it, as needed.

"We're quite a team," Quinn says proudly as we finish up our training session for the day, leaning down to kiss me on the cheek. We've been in Bloodstone Castle for two nights and I have yet to see my Aunt Saxe. I just… I haven't been ready to face her and Maura LeChance has been keeping us very busy as she's filled us in on the happenings regarding the other Chosen and we've told her about everything we've been through, as well.

Maura hasn't questioned me about my Aunt Saxe,

the Blue Faerie, or when I'd like to see her. I'm fairly
sure she's waiting for me to approach her with the
request.

"Yes, we are," Peter adds, kissing my other cheek.

We join hands and walk down one of the many
pathways that lead around the castle and through the
gardens, content to be together and share all that we
have, no matter how bad it might have gotten for any of
us. I'm convinced this is what happiness feels like.

"Well, the three of you look positively blissful,"
Maura says as we walk past her, where she stands on
the grass, overseeing a young Fae who is doing her own
training.

"Oh, Maura. I need to speak to you about
something," I say before addressing Peter and Quinn.
"I'll see the two of you later?"

"You certainly will," Peter replies as they continue
on, chuckling about something. I step closer to Maura
and give her a big smile as she watches my men leave.

"Quite the men you have there, Tinker," she says
as she turns back to face me.

"Yes, they are pretty wonderful," I agree, watching
them fondly.

"What did you need to talk to me about?" she asks,
facing me expectantly. But there's something in her
eyes that says she already knows.

I take a breath, dreading the subject even as it
comes to my tongue. "I'd like to speak to my Aunt
Saxe. Can you tell me where I can find her?" I dread
the idea of seeing my aunt because I'm not sure how

she'll respond to me—will she be angry over what I've done? Will she understand it was just an accident and that I never intended to kill her? Will she understand that it was Morningstar's influence or which she blame me for not being able to control the evil within me? I don't know and I'm afraid to find out.

"I'll do you one better," Maura answers. "I'll take you to her," she finishes, motioning for her student to cease her lessons. The student does as Maura instructs and then leaves us to our solitude.

"Are you ready?" Maura asks with a beaming smile.

I feel nothing but anxiety. Even so, I am ready.

I nod and follow her down a long and winding path that leads through the small town surrounding Bloodstone Castle and through the forest that borders it. We walk in silence, single-file, weaving this way and that, underneath the heavy canopy of tree branches. When we arrive in front of a small cottage, Maura stops walking and turns to face me.

"You'll find the Blue Faerie in there.'

"Thank you," I reply, watching Maura walk away before I dare face the front door. I stand, rooted in place, unable to move for a few seconds. My heart thunders through my body, and I prepare myself for a potentially uncomfortable situation. I take another deep breath and walk up to the door, knocking gently as I expect the worst. But, it's time I faced the music.

The door is opens lazily and I find myself greeted by the smiling face of my aunt, well… more a faded version of it. Though my Aunt Saxe stands in front of me, she's more vision than physical entity. I can see through her, to the other side of her humble house, and I wonder if she's a ghost? I'm not exactly sure how to ask though.

"Tinker, my lovely girl!" she says as she throws her arms wide and I feel tears break through my eyes immediately. Even though she can't hold me, owing to the fact that she's basically transparent, the attempt isn't lost on me.

"Aunt Saxe," I whisper.

She pulls away and just looks at me, and there's pride in her eyes. "It's been so long since I've seen you," she says as I glance down at my shoes bashfully. I'm not even sure what to say or what to do.

"I'm… I'm sorry, Aunt Saxe, I'm so sorry."

She immediately shushes me. "There's nothing to be sorry for, dear girl."

"There's *everything* to be sorry for."

But, she shakes her head. "Everything is as it was meant to be. You must always remember that. The things that happen—they are out of our control but they are meant to be, all the same."

"I don't… understand how you can be so… okay with things."

"Because I understand," she says simply, her smile never fading. "Now, tell me how you are."

I breathe in deeply as she welcomes me into her small, yet comfy house. "I don't even know where… to start."

210

"You seem troubled."

"I am." After taking in my surroundings, I turn to face her. "I came here to apologize, Aunt Saxe."

"You already have, dear."

I shake my head. "No, it's not enough. I came to… to explain what happened and how I never intended…" I lose my nerve and look away from her, my lower lip trembling. "I'm… I'm so sorry for what happened. I never meant to do this to you." I motion to her and the fact that I can basically see through her. "Whatever *this* is. I don't understand how you're even here…" I take another breath. "I never intended for any of this to ever happen and when it did… I've never forgiven myself. It's something I've thought about night and day."

"I never believed for a moment that you intended to harm me. It was just an unfortunate event, that's all."

"Can you forgive me?"

"There's nothing to forgive. I never blamed you, Tinker. It's not your fault."

"It is my fault," I reply, tears falling down my face.

"No, you lost control and you didn't understand your own magic or the power of Morningstar within your veins."

That much is true and I can't argue it. Instead, I close my eyes against the memories, against the pain and I can feel her gaze on me, even with my eyes closed. Her magic embraces me as she surrounds me in a hug. I linger in her arms, releasing the pent-up pain that has been with me for so long, letting the tears fall. I let go of the pain of what I did to her all those years

211

ago. I release the shame and the guilt. I let go of the pain of losing my wing. I try to let go of the fear I feel inside, but it still lingers.

"There is something more..." she says, clearly reading my emotions.

I nod as I pull away from her. "How will I ever defeat Septimus?" I ask her. "He's so much stronger than I am and he's taken so much from me already. I'm no match for his magic or cruelty." I look over my shoulder. "And now I can't even fly."

"You have no need to match his evil heart, dear. Your heart is good, pure. You have a tender heart and that is in no way a weakness. It is your love, light and loyalty that will defeat Septimus, Tinker. Those are the three things he will never understand, the three things he'll never be able to defend himself against because he possesses none of them."

"Can you see how it will end?"

"No," she says and shakes her head. "I'm afraid no one is privy to knowing the future, my love. But I can see the strength in you and that strength will only grow as you prepare for the battle that is to come. You have everything you need to be the victor, Tinker. You must just believe in yourself."

"Thank you," I reply, wiping away the wetness from my face.

"Never doubt yourself, Tinker. You are far more powerful than you know. You must embrace that fact and never forget it."

"I will," I tell her.

"Now go and think no longer on the pain of the past. It's done and gone and there's nothing you can do about it now. Instead, focus on the future and on your happiness," she says, smiling broadly at me as I lose to another round of tears. I just don't understand how she doesn't begrudge me, doesn't bear any anger over what happened between us.

"Enjoy your life and the wonderful men Maura tells me you've brought into it. There are beautiful things in the future for all of you."

I smile and nod as I turn and walk out the door. The sun shines down on me as I step outside. I can feel its warmth and its power and it seems to fill whatever void was within me previously. Perhaps I am like the sun, but on a smaller scale. I like that thought, and I hold it in my heart as I hear the soft pitter-patter of feet behind me.

I turn and watch my Aunt Saxe as she smiles at me and then snaps the fingers on one of her hands. And it's then I feel an incredible burst of heat from my back, as though the sun has been warming it for hours. I glance back and see my missing wing suddenly returned, flapping in time with the other.

Pixie dust glitters through the air as I face my Aunt Saxe and smile more broadly than I ever have before. She returns the expression and then returns to her little cottage in the middle of nowhere.

EPILOGUE
AMIES

"You need to find the record keeper," the small wood sprite tells me as I enter the office of cartography.

"Where would I find this person?" I ask.

"Down the hall, second door. If not there, then you'll have to ask around. We've been terribly busy around here since Tinkerbell banished her uncle, Septimus, from Sweetland. Lots of rebuilding and rezoning taking place to fix the mess he and Agatha turned this place into."

"I can imagine. Okay. Thanks," I tell him, heading back out the door and making my way down the hall.

I've been entrusted with a map drawn by the Blue Faerie, but I can't make out anything on it. It's all written in some sort of code, a cypher developed by the Blue Faerie when she created it, just in case it was taken by someone unworthy of the information it contained or the Unseelie tunneled into her dead brain to try to retrieve the information.

"Are you the record keeper?" I ask of a honey-haired young woman sitting inside the room I've been directed to by the sprite.

"No."

"Can you tell me where to find him?"

214

"Her."

"Excuse me?"

"*Her.* The person you're looking for is a *her*, not a *him*."

"Ah, I see. Very well. Can you tell me where I might find *her* then?"

"No."

Frustrated, I turn to leave, not sure where I'm supposed to find the person I need to speak to, but then I turn back again. "I need to speak to someone who can decipher a map for me. Is there someone else here who can do that?"

"No."

"Thank you. You've been extremely helpful," I snarl, turning to leave. Much to my surprise, a small gnome wanders out from behind another counter and addresses me.

"Don't mind Esmie. She's had a rough week and isn't exactly in good spirits. I'm headed out to retrieve some of the new gumdrops being brought in to reseed the field. If you wish to walk with me, I can take you to the person you wish to see."

"And who is that?"

"Ember Limus."

A name—at last. This trip might actually yield something positive, after all. "Very good. Thank you."

"You're welcome."

I follow along behind the gnome, taking painfully short steps due to his small stature. It seems to take forever just to go three buildings, but we finally arrive in front of a cottage-house made of chocolate chip cookies joined together by white chocolate beams. He motions toward it once we stop in front.

"Ember is in there."

"Thank you for your help."

"Anytime," he replies before meandering down the path.

I knock on the door, and it opens slightly. I wait a few more seconds, but no one makes an appearance, so I knock again, opening the door another few inches. Still no response. Hoping nothing unfortunate has happened to the woman I've come to see, I push the door open and step inside, surprised to find an interior much larger than it would appear from the outside. There's a receptionist sitting at a desk made of pixie sticks and gumdrops. I'm surprised to see her, as I assumed the abode was a private home and yet it looks nothing like a home on the inside, and everything like a business of some sort.

The receptionist sits on an extremely high chair with a set of small stairs to one side of her. The desk and the chair are full size, but she's hardly bigger than a cricket.

"Can I help you?" she asks into a bullhorn that only manages to make her tiny voice barely audible.

"Yes, I'm looking for Ember Limus," I tell her.

"She's not here," she replies.

"Do you know where I can find her?"

"No."

I sigh loudly. With the exception of the helpful

gnome, the citizens of Sweetland are not very friendly. I turn on my toes, ready to leave the strange building, when someone from behind me clears her throat.

"You're looking for me?" she asks.

"Are you Ember Limus?" I reply as I turn around.

"I am," she says, but I'm unable to respond.

Instead, I just stand there for a moment, completely spellbound by the most beautiful woman I've ever seen. After a few moments of awkward silence, she prods me again.

"Are you looking for me or aren't you?" she asks, seeming more than a bit amused.

"I, uh. Yes, I am looking for you."

She smiles more broadly, revealing perfectly white teeth amid the pinkest lips I've ever seen on a woman. And there's not a touch of falsity about them. They're as natural as her deep blue eyes and her gold hair.

"And who might you be?" she asks.

I'm suddenly embarrassed as I remember myself. "I'm Amies Padmoore."

"And why have you come, Amies Padmoore?"

I find this woman quite perplexing, though I'm not certain why. "I've been told you're the best cartographer in the land."

"That would be accurate."

"Very good," I say as I take a deep breath and wonder what the blasted hell has gotten into me. Ordinarily, I'm never flustered in front of a lovely woman. "I need your help with a map given to me by the Blue Faerie."

Now it's her turn to seem stunned. She hesitates for a moment, looking from me to the scroll rolled beneath my arm, and then waves toward a door to one side of the lobby.

"Well, then let's have a look, shall we?"

To Be Continued in
EMBER

Now Available!

DOWNLOAD FREE EBOOKS!
It's as easy as:

1. Visit my website (hpmallory.com)

2. Sign up in the popup box or the link on the home page

3. Check your email!

HP MALLORY is a New York Times and USA Today Bestselling Author!

She lives in Southern California with her son, where she is at work on her next book.

Printed in Great Britain
by Amazon

82805704R00132